The Demon Headmaster

Gillian Cross worked in a school and a bakery before
studying at Oxford and Sussex universities. She has also
been a childminder and an assistant to an MP. She has
written around thirty books for children, many of them
published in Puffin. In 1991 she was awarded the Carnegie
Medal for *Wolf* and has won both the Smarties Prize and
the Whitbread Award for *The Great Elephant Chase*.
Gillian Cross lives in Warwickshire with her husband
and two of their four children. Her hobbies are orienteer-
ing and playing the piano.

Once you have finished reading *The Demon Headmaster*
you may be interested in reading the Afterword by Chris
Powling on page 141.

Other books by Gillian Cross

THE PRIME MINISTER'S BRAIN
THE REVENGE OF THE DEMON HEADMASTER
THE DEMON HEADMASTER STRIKES AGAIN

THE GREAT ELEPHANT CHASE
NEW WORLD
ON THE EDGE
ROSCOE'S LEAP
TWIN AND SUPER-TWIN
WOLF
THE ROMAN BEANFEAST

For older readers

CHARTBREAK

For younger readers

RENT-A-GENIUS

GILLIAN CROSS

The Demon Headmaster

ILLUSTRATED BY KENNY McKENDRY

PUFFIN BOOKS

in association with Oxford University Press

PUFFIN BOOKS

Published by the Penguin Group
Penguin Books Ltd, 27 Wrights Lane, London W8 5TZ, England
Penguin Putnam Inc., 375 Hudson Street, New York, New York 10014, USA
Penguin Books Australia Ltd, Ringwood, Victoria, Australia
Penguin Books Canada Ltd, 10 Alcorn Avenue, Toronto, Ontario, Canada M4V 3B2
Penguin Books (NZ) Ltd, Private Bag 102902, NSMC, Auckland, New Zealand

Penguin Books Ltd, Registered Offices: Harmondsworth, Middlesex, England

First published by Oxford University Press 1982
Published in Puffin Books 1984
Published in Puffin Modern Classics 1997
Published in this edition 1998
1 3 5 7 9 10 8 6 4 2

Set in Bembo

Made and printed in England by Clays Ltd, St Ives plc

ISBN 0–141–30369–7

Contents

CHAPTER I

A Girl in the House

'Our last moments of freedom,' Lloyd said darkly. He glowered round the battered walls of the playroom, at the motorbike posters peeling off the wallpaper and Harvey's model aeroplanes neatly ranged on top of the bookcase. 'She'll be sticking up pictures of flowers and ballet dancers when she comes, I bet.'

He mooched about gloomily, kicking at the furniture. '"Take care of her," Mum said. What does she expect us to do? Hold her hand and tell her bedtime stories?'

Harvey, curled in his chair, stolidly went on reading *The Aeromodeller*.

'H!' Lloyd banged him crossly on the shoulder. 'Why don't you say something?'

Harvey looked up and grinned. 'You've gone all red in the face.'

That only made Lloyd angrier. 'Red in the face? I should just think I have. Purple pancakes! Don't you realize how awful it'll be? Having a girl come to live here!'

'But you've known for ages,' Harvey said mildly. 'Mum's always wanted to have someone to foster.'

'I thought she meant a baby,' Lloyd spluttered. 'That would have been OK. Just a bit of screaming at night. But a girl! A wretched girl, as old as me! She'll never be out of our hair. We'll have to take her to *school* with us.'

'So?' Harvey shrugged. 'Might be a good thing. She might be on our side. Another Normal.'

Lloyd looked at him scornfully. 'Is it likely? I ask you. There's only five of us in the whole school. No, she'll be one of *them*. And what about the others? What will they say?'

'Have to wait and see, won't we?' Harvey picked up his magazine again. Enraged, Lloyd leaped across and knocked it out of his hands. 'Harvey Hunter, you're an *idiot*! Can't you see what it means? We'll have a little goody-goody about the place all the time, going on about how wonderful school is, and how marvellous the Headmaster is. I can't bear it. It'll be like having a spy in the house.'

For a moment, Harvey looked troubled. Then he brightened. 'Might not be as bad as that. If she watches us, we could watch her too.' A distant expression came over his face. 'You never know. We might actually be able to discover something. Find out what's going on.'

Lloyd stopped pacing the room and stared coldly at him. 'I've told you a hundred times,' he hissed, 'that's crazy. It'll just get us into trouble. We've worked out a good system for having a quiet life. I don't want anyone interfering with it.'

'But don't you ever *wonder*?' Harvey said dreamily. 'I do. In the afternoons. I sit and stare across at the Hall and wonder what the rest of them are doing, and why they're so –'

'Shut up!' Lloyd caught him by the shoulder and shook him hard. 'I've managed to keep you out of real trouble ever since you came to the school. And jolly difficult it's been. Four years of watching and being careful. I won't have you mucking everything up now. You just behave yourself and –'

'OK, OK.' Scarlet in the face from the shaking, Harvey held up a hand to push Lloyd away. 'Keep your hair on. You don't want to be looking like a raging demon when she gets here.' Coolly he picked up his magazine and started to read again. Lloyd stared at him in disgust.

'Just wish I *did* look like a demon. That might frighten her away.' And he resumed his restless, furious pacing round the room.

'They're such a nice, *normal* family,' Miss Wilberforce said encouragingly, as the car jerked to a stop at the traffic lights. 'I'm sure you'll like living with them, Dinah. Lloyd and Harvey, the two boys, are very sensible and ordinary. It's a pity you couldn't meet them beforehand, but I'm sure you'll get on.'

'Yes, Miss Wilberforce,' Dinah said woodenly.

'Of course, it's hard on you, having to change schools. I hope you won't find the work too difficult. You'll just have to put your back into it.'

'Yes, Miss Wilberforce.'

Miss Wilberforce sighed and looked round at her, taking one hand off the steering wheel. 'You don't seem very relaxed, dear. Are you, perhaps, just a teeny bit afraid? Mmm?'

'No, Miss Wilberforce.'

Miss Wilberforce sighed again. 'Hmm. Oh well, we're here now.' She steered the car in towards the kerb. 'Let's go in and meet them all.'

'Yes, Miss Wilberforce.' Dinah climbed out and stood stiffly on the pavement while Miss Wilberforce got her case out of the boot. Then the two of them marched up the front path of the Hunters' house and Miss Wilberforce rang the doorbell.

'Don't worry if you feel a bit strange at first,' she whispered. 'They'll do their best to make you at home.'

The door opened.

'Dinah, dear, how nice to see you again,' Mrs Hunter said. She held out her arms and gave Dinah a friendly hug and kiss. Dinah's body stayed quite stiff.

'Hallo, Mrs Hunter. Hallo, Mr Hunter,' she said, without expression.

'Come in and take your coat off. The boys are dying to meet you.'

'Oh,' said Dinah.

'I'm sure Dinah's looking forward to meeting them, too,' Miss Wilberforce put in quickly. 'But she's bound to be a bit shy, aren't you, dear?'

'No,' said Dinah.

Mr Hunter grinned at her. 'At least you know your own mind. Go into the living room. I'll call the boys.'

Dinah went in and sat on the edge of the sofa, with her knees pressed together. Her eyes flicked from side to side of the room. It was just what she had expected. Three-piece suite. Television. A shelf of ornaments. A very ordinary room. She sighed softly. Then she sat up straighter as everyone else came in.

'Here they are,' Mrs Hunter said proudly. 'Lloyd's the big one, and Harvey's the little fat one.'

'Cheek!' Harvey protested amiably.

Dinah looked them up and down. Lloyd was taller than she was, with a mop of wild hair and a cocky look. Harvey was roly-poly and cheerful. There did not seem to be anything special about either of them. She held out a cold, rigid hand.

'Hallo,' she said unenthusiastically.

CHAPTER 2

Not a Good Beginning

'Hallo,' Lloyd said back, just as unenthusiastically. He stared down at her hand, but he did not take it. She was even worse than he had expected. A pale, pinched face and two stringy plaits. Crimson cabbages, she looked just like a wooden doll.

She gazed awkwardly at the two of them, and they gazed back.

'I'll tell you what,' Mrs Hunter said briskly. 'I'm sure you'll get on better without a lot of grown-ups breathing down your necks. Why don't you boys grab some tea from the kitchen and take Dinah into the playroom? Then you can get to know each other properly. Off you go.'

With excessive politeness, Lloyd held the door open for Dinah while Harvey went out to the kitchen for some food. A few moments later, the three of them were sitting round the playroom table silently eating sandwiches.

'Have another cheese sandwich, Dinah?' Lloyd held out the plate.

'No thank you.'

'How about peanut butter?' Harvey said helpfully.

'No thank you.'

'Another glass of Coke?' Lloyd picked up the bottle.

'No thank you.'

With a sudden snort, Lloyd exploded. 'That's all you've said so far. "Yes please". "No thank you". What are you? A robot?'

'Perhaps she's shy,' Harvey said kindly.

'Well?' Lloyd looked at her. 'Are you shy?'

'No,' Dinah said.

'Go on then.' Lloyd prodded her. '*Say* something. Tell us about yourself.'

Dinah drew a breath. 'My name is Dinah Glass. I'm eleven. My mother and father died when I was one. I've lived in the Children's Home for ten years.' Her mouth snapped shut again.

'Suffering crumpets!' Lloyd made another clutch at his chaotic hair. 'She *is* a robot.'

Harvey smiled at her encouragingly. 'No she's not. Go on, Dinah. Say some more. Aren't there any questions you want to ask us?'

Dinah sat for a moment, frowning slightly while she considered. Then she said, 'Tell me about the school.'

'I told you, H, I *told* you!' Lloyd rolled his eyes dramatically upwards and banged the table. 'That's all she's interested in. Rotten school! It's going to be terrible.'

Dinah looked at him coldly. 'What's the matter?'

'What's the matter?' Lloyd jumped up, knocking his chair sideways. 'What's the *matter*? Scarlet sausages, why should I want to talk about school when I'm not there? You'd think anyone would be glad to escape for a day or two and not have to think about –' He paused, panting for breath.

'He doesn't like our school,' Harvey said.

'So I see,' Dinah said. 'Why not?'

Lloyd looked craftily at her. 'Guess. What's the worst thing you can imagine in a school?'

With one finger, Dinah rubbed the end of her nose thoughtfully. 'Chaos. Children running round shouting everywhere, and nobody keeping any order.'

Lloyd gave a loud bellow of laughter and Harvey grinned and shook his head. 'Nothing like that. Try again.'

Dinah frowned. 'Vandalism? Kids smashing everything up?'

Harvey giggled, and Lloyd looked scornfully at her. 'You haven't got a clue. Not a clue. Just you wait until Monday. It won't be at all the way you expect.' He reached forward and switched on the television.

'You're not going to tell?' Dinah said.

'Nope,' Lloyd said annoyingly. 'Don't want to go on talking about school for ever, do I? Anyway, can't you see what time it is?'

Dinah glanced round at the clock. 'Six o'clock. But what does that –'

'Don't know what six o'clock on Friday means?' Lloyd sniffed. 'Didn't they watch the Eddy Hair Show at your Children's Home then?'

'Oh. Yes.' Dinah shrugged. 'I just forgot.'

'Good thing Lloyd remembered,' Harvey said. 'We don't want to miss the Great School Quiz at the end of the programme, because – OUCH!'

Lloyd had given him a sharp kick. 'Will you *shut up* about school, H!'

'So I can't even ask *him* about it?' Dinah said stiffly.

With an irritating grin, Lloyd wagged his finger at her. 'Got you guessing? *That's* how I like it!'

The television screen flickered and then a picture swam into focus. A man with long purple hair and a purple-painted face was standing on his head, waggling his feet at the camera. 'Got you guessing?' he said chirpily. '*That's* how I like it.'

Dinah pulled a face at the screen. 'I think Eddy Hair's stupid. And you're even more stupid, Lloyd Hunter. I'll find out about your daft school on Monday.'

For the rest of the weekend, Dinah avoided Lloyd and Harvey even harder than they avoided her. Whenever Mrs Hunter sent them up to play with her, she was curled on her bed, reading a book and not wanting to be disturbed. They hardly spoke to her again until Monday morning. Then, when they clattered down the stairs, late for breakfast, she was already sitting at the table, neat and prim in a white blouse and a blue skirt and jumper. Lloyd stared at her.

'What's that you're wearing?'

'School uniform.' She smoothed her skirt. 'From my old school.'

Harvey was looking worried. 'The Headmaster won't like it.' He sat down and heaped sugar on to his porridge. 'All green, he likes. We all have to be green.'

'Or else,' Lloyd said with relish.

Dinah ate her last spoonful of porridge and folded her napkin precisely. 'Or else what?'

'You'll see,' Lloyd muttered darkly. 'Pass the sugar, H. We don't want to be late.'

'Or else?' said Dinah sweetly. She looked at them over her cup as she drank her tea. 'Scared?'

'I'm not scared of anyone,' Lloyd blustered. 'Not even the Headmaster.'

'Bet you are,' Dinah said.

'Bet I'm not.'

Dinah smiled annoyingly.

'*I* am,' Harvey said calmly. 'I'd be a fool if I wasn't. He —'

'Shut up!' Lloyd said sharply. 'Don't tell her a thing. Let her find it all out for herself.' He went on eating his porridge.

Harvey spooned his breakfast quickly into his mouth. He still had not finished when Mrs Hunter bustled in.

'Hurry up, hurry up.' She flapped round the room. 'You'll all be late if you don't go in five minutes. I wish I could come with you, Dinah dear, but the gas man's coming and I daren't go out. We'll freeze to death if we don't get the central heating mended soon.'

'That's all right,' Dinah said politely.

'I've written a letter to the Headmaster, and the boys will take care of you. They know – oh Harvey, do get your coat on!'

Shoving and nagging, she pushed them out of the front door and they walked up the road in an awkward threesome. Dinah was on the outside so that she had to step into the gutter, trailing her feet through frosty leaves, whenever they passed anyone. Lloyd kept as far away from her as he could and watched her carefully out of the corner of his eye.

As they approached the school, they began to see groups of children, all neatly dressed in green with white shirts and striped ties. They walked sedately along the pavement, without laughing or joking, and Dinah looked at them curiously.

'Funny,' she said. 'Don't they play or fight or anything on the way to school?'

'Never,' Lloyd said shortly. As the school came in sight, he and Harvey fell into step, marching with their eyes straight ahead.

'Faster,' Harvey said anxiously. 'I've got to take the registers round. Remember? The Headmaster told me on Friday.'

Lloyd groaned. 'Why didn't you say, you idiot? You'll be late.'

'We could run,' murmured Dinah.

'No we couldn't,' snapped Lloyd. 'No one runs.'

She opened her mouth to say something and then shut it again as they reached the school gates. Without any comment, all the children had stopped. Taking combs out of their pockets, they combed their hair neatly, put their hats straight and smoothed their ties. Dinah stared. Lloyd was dragging a comb through his unruly curls and Harvey twitched nervously at the lapels of his blazer.

'Will I do? He won't complain?'

'You're fine.' Lloyd clapped him on the back. 'Perfect. And I think you've just got enough time for the registers. Go in and do it as quietly as you can, so no one notices you started late.'

With a nod, Harvey plodded round to the playground, behind the school, and began to walk up the steps into the building. Dinah glanced at him as she and Lloyd followed.

'Why was he worried? I thought he was quite tidy *before* he combed his hair.'

'You would,' muttered Lloyd. 'You don't understand. I just hope he gets the registers out without trouble.'

'Why should there be any *trouble* about *registers*?' Dinah sniffed. 'That's silly.'

Lloyd opened his mouth to answer her, but before he could say anything a tall, fair-haired boy came slouching across the playground towards them. He did not seem in any hurry, but as soon as he was close to Lloyd he whispered, with great urgency, 'Quick! What was Harvey doing, going into school? I tried to catch his eye, but he didn't see me.'

'That's OK, Ian,' Lloyd said. 'He's gone in to do registers.'

'Registers?' Ian's face did not change from its casual, cheerful expression, but his voice sounded horrified. 'No he's not. Rose came out and told Sharon to do them, because it was so late. She said the Headmaster wouldn't have anyone else in there before school started.'

'Oh no!' Lloyd gasped. 'Orange onions with silver skins! I'd better go in and try to get him out before anyone sees him.'

'It won't matter, surely?' Dinah said. 'If anyone sees him, they'll just send him out again.'

Lloyd and Ian looked contemptuously at her. 'You'll see,' Lloyd said. 'Here.' He fished his mother's letter out of his pocket. 'Take this. I've got to go and look for Harvey.'

Without another word he was off, hurrying up the steps into the school. Ian turned away and Dinah was left standing all alone in the playground, shivering in the bitter, wintry wind. She looked thoughtfully up at the school. At one window, she could see a motionless figure, in a green blazer with a large white P sewn on to one pocket. It was gazing through the window, but not at her. Its eyes were fixed on the steps up which Harvey and then Lloyd had just hurried. Dinah stared at it for a moment and then, with a shrug, turned back to the playground.

CHAPTER 3

The Headmaster

*I*t was a big playground, full of groups of strange children. No one so much as glanced at Dinah and she felt very awkward. But she was not a person who showed her feelings. Her pinched mouth did not relax for a moment. She looked round, wondering if there were any games she could join in. She thought there would be football, skipping and He. And lots of people shouting and telling the latest crazy jokes from Friday night's Eddy Hair Show.

But it was not like that at all. All the children were standing in small neat circles in different parts of the playground, muttering. Carefully Dinah sidled up to the first circle, trying to catch what the voices were saying. When she heard, she could hardly believe it.

'Nine twenty-ones are a hundred and eighty-nine,

Ten twenty-ones are two hundred and ten,

Eleven twenty-ones are two hundred and thirty-one . . .'

Extraordinary! She left them to it and moved across to another group, wondering if they were doing something more interesting. But they seemed to be reciting too. Only what they were saying was different.

'William the First 1066 to 1087,

William the Second 1087 to 1100,

Henry the First 1100 to 1135 . . .'

She stood beside them for some time, but they did not waver or look round at her. They just went on chanting, their faces earnest. Behind her she could hear a third group. There, the children were muttering the names of the capitals of different countries.

'The capital of France is Paris,

The capital of Spain is Madrid,

The capital of the United States is –'

'New York,' said a little girl's voice.

'Lucy!' A bigger girl took her by the shoulder and shook her. 'You know that's not right. Come on, quickly. What is it?'

'I can't – I can't remember,' Lucy said in a scared voice. 'You know I've been away. Tell me. Please, Julie.'

'You know we're not supposed to tell you if you haven't learnt it,' Julie said crossly. 'Now come on. The capital of the United States is –'

Miserably, Lucy chewed at her bottom lip and shook her head from side to side. 'I can't remember.'

The whole circle of children was looking accusingly at her and Dinah was suddenly annoyed with them for being so smug. Stepping forwards, she whispered in Lucy's ear, 'It's Washington DC.'

'The capital of the United States is Washington DC,' Lucy gabbled, with a quick, grateful smile.

From the rest of the circle, cold, disapproving eyes glared at Dinah. *Never be too clever*, she thought. *I should've known that.* Her face pinched up tight again as she stepped back and heard them start up once more. 'The capital of Russia is Moscow. The capital of Brazil is –'

Woodenly, Dinah walked on round the playground, waiting for the bell to ring or the whistle to go.

But there was no bell. No whistle. Nothing. Instead, quite abruptly, all sounds in the playground stopped and the children turned round to stare at the school.

There on the steps stood a row of six children, three boys and three girls. They were all tall and heavily built and they were marked out from the others by a large white P sewn on to their blazer pockets. Without smiling, the tallest girl took a pace forwards.

'Form – rows!' she yelled into the silence.

'Yes, Rose,' all the children said, in perfect unison. As quietly and steadily as marching soldiers, they walked together, forming neat straight lines which ran the length of the playground. Each child stood exactly a foot behind the one in front. Each line was exactly three feet from the one next to it. Not quite sure what to do, Dinah stood by herself, a blotch of blue among the green.

The tallest boy on the steps walked forwards.

'Lead – in!' he bellowed.

'Yes, Jeff,' chorused the children.

Still in total silence, they began to march forward, row by row, up the steps and through the door into the school, their eyes fixed straight ahead and their feet moving in step. There was no giggling or whispering or pushing. The whole thing was utterly orderly, the only sound being the steady tramping of feet.

Dinah continued to stand still, watching, until the playground was almost clear. As the last line marched off, she tacked herself on to the end of it and walked towards the school. When she got to the top of the steps, Rose stuck out an arm, barring her way.

'Name?' she said briskly.

'Dinah Glass,' Dinah said. 'I'm new, and –'

'Just answer the questions,' Jeff interrupted her. 'What's that you're wearing?'

'It's my old school uniform. I –'

'Just answer the question,' he said again. There was no friendliness in his voice and as he spoke he looked not at Dinah but over her shoulder. 'It is not satisfactory. All pupils here shall wear correct green uniform. Kindly see to it.'

He looked so haughty and spoke so stiffly that Dinah was irritated.

'I don't know why you're being so bossy,' she said coldly. 'Anyone'd think you were one of the teachers, instead of a measly kid like anyone else.'

'All pupils shall obey the prefects,' chanted Rose, in the same stiff voice. 'The prefects are the voice of the Headmaster,'

Dinah felt puzzled, but she was determined not to show it. She thrust her chin up and looked straight at them. 'Well, I think you should take me to see the Headmaster. I've got a letter for him.'

The prefects looked doubtfully at each other. Then Jeff vanished inside the school, while the others stood barring Dinah's way. It had grown colder and the icy wind was turning her fingers blue. She lifted them to blow on them.

'Hands by your sides,' Rose rapped out instantly. 'Good deportment is the sign of an orderly mind.'

Stubbornly, Dinah went on blowing. At once, Rose said, 'Sarah! Simon!'

Dinah's hands were instantly seized by two of the other prefects, who forced them down to her sides and stood holding them like that until Jeff reappeared.

'The Headmaster will see you,' he said. 'Follow me.'

Thoroughly bewildered now, Dinah walked into the school after him and along a straight corridor. At her old school, all the walls had been covered with pictures and drawings done by the pupils, but these walls were completely blank, except for a framed notice hung half-way along. Dinah swivelled her head to read it as she passed.

The man who can keep order can rule the world.

Frowning slightly, she went on following Jeff until he

came to a stop in front of a door which had the single word HEADMASTER painted on it.

He knocked.

'Come in.'

Jeff pushed the door open and waved Dinah inside, pulling it shut behind her.

As she stepped through, Dinah glanced quickly round the room. It was the tidiest office she had ever seen. There were no papers, no files, no pictures on the walls. Just a large, empty-topped desk, a filing cabinet and a bookcase with a neat row of books.

She took it all in in one second and then forgot it as her eyes fell on the man standing by the window. He was tall and thin, dressed in an immaculate black suit. From his shoulders, a long, black teacher's gown hung in heavy folds, like wings, giving him the appearance of a huge crow. Only his head was startlingly white. Fair hair, almost as colourless as snow, lay round a face with paper-white skin and pallid lips. His eyes were hidden behind dark glasses, like two black holes in the middle of all the whiteness.

She cleared her throat. 'Hallo. I'm Dinah Glass and I –'

He raised a long, ivory-coloured hand. 'Please do not speak until you are asked. Idle chatter is an inefficient waste of energy.'

Unnervingly, he went on staring at her for a moment or two without saying anything else. Dinah wished she could see the eyes behind the dark lenses. With his eyes hidden, his expression was unreadable.

Finally, he waved a hand towards an upright chair, pulled round to face the desk. 'Sit down.' He sat down himself, facing her, and pulled a sheet of paper out of a drawer.

'Dinah Glass,' he said crisply, writing it down in neat, precise script. 'You are being fostered by Mrs Hunter?'

Dinah nodded.

'Answer properly, please.'

'Yes, sir.'

'And why is she not here, to introduce you?'

'She couldn't come, but she's sent you a letter.'

Reaching across the desk, the Headmaster twitched it out of her hand and slit the envelope with a small steel paper knife. As he read the letter, Dinah settled herself more comfortably, expecting to be asked a string of questions.

But there were no questions. Instead, he pushed a sheet of paper across the desk towards her. 'This is a test,' he said. 'It is given to all new pupils.'

'Haven't you got a report on me?' Dinah said. 'From my other school?'

'No one else's reports are of any use to me,' said the Headmaster. 'Please be quiet and do the test.'

His voice was low, but somehow rather frightening. Dinah took a pen out of her pocket and looked down at the paper.

The questions were fairly hard. Mostly sums, with a bit of English thrown in and one or two brain-teasers. She knew that most children would have found them difficult to answer and she paused for a moment, working out where she was going to make her deliberate mistakes. Not too many. Just enough to avoid trouble.

Then she picked up the pen and began to write. As she scribbled, she could feel him watching her and every time she glanced up he was the same. Pale and motionless, with two black circles where his eyes should have been. She was so nervous that she stumbled once or twice, getting some of the answers right where she had meant to make mistakes. To keep the balance, she had to botch up all the last three questions. Not very good. It did not look as convincing as it should have done. Her hand trembled slightly as she passed the paper back across the table.

The Headmaster scanned it carefully for a moment, then looked up at her.

'You are an intelligent girl.'

Dinah's heart sank, but, with an effort, she kept her face calm, meeting the Headmaster's gaze steadily. At last, he said, 'But you make too many mistakes. I wonder —' He chewed for a moment on his bottom lip. Then he shrugged. 'It doesn't matter. I dare say we shall find out all about you in due course.'

She looked down to the floor, trying not to seem too relieved, and waiting to be told which class she should go to. But the Headmaster did not seem in any hurry to get rid of her. He crumpled the test paper in his hand and dropped it into the rubbish bin. Then, slowly, he reached up a hand to take off his glasses.

Dinah found herself shivering. Ridiculously, she expected him to have pink eyes, because the rest of his face was so colourless. Or perhaps no eyes at all . . .

But his eyes were not pink. They were large and luminous, and a peculiar sea-green colour. She had never seen eyes like them before, and she found herself staring into them. Staring and staring.

'Funny you should be so tired,' he said, softly. 'So early in the morning.'

She opened her mouth to say that she was not tired, but, to her surprise, she yawned instead.

'*So* tired,' crooned the Headmaster, his huge, extraordinary eyes fixed on her face. 'You can hardly move your arms and legs. You are so tired, so tired. You feel your head begin to nod and slowly, slowly your eyes are starting to close. *So* tired and sleepy.'

He's mad, Dinah thought muzzily. *The whole school's raving mad*. But she felt her eyes start to close, in spite of all she could do. She was drifting, drifting . . . All she could see was two pools, deep green like the sea, and she seemed to sink into them as she drifted off and off . . .

She opened her eyes again and gave a nervous laugh. 'I'm sorry. What did you say?'

'You fell asleep,' the Headmaster said coldly. 'You have been asleep for a long time.' He put his glasses on again.

'Asleep?' Dinah stared.

'For the whole morning.'

She looked at him in bewilderment and then glanced round at the clock on the wall. To her amazement, the hands pointed to twelve o'clock. 'But I don't understand.'

'Perhaps you should go to bed earlier,' he said, with a strange smile. 'Now go and have some dinner. The dining hall is at the end of this corridor. After dinner, you will go into the Hall with Class One.'

Still puzzled, Dinah nodded.

The Headmaster looked disagreeably at her. 'Your uniform,' he said, 'is not what I require.'

'It's what I had for my other school. When I was at the Children's Home.'

His lips narrowed. 'I dislike argument. It serves no useful purpose. You will appear in the correct school uniform by next Monday. I am sending a list to Mrs Hunter to ensure that she buys the proper items. I like to see all my pupils dressed in an orderly manner.' His voice rose a tone. 'I will not *endure* disorder. It is inefficient. Now go and have some dinner.'

Shakily, Dinah stood up and made for the door. As she reached out her hand for the handle, the Headmaster spoke again.

'I have put you in the same class as Lloyd Hunter, but I wish you to have as little as possible to do with Lloyd and Harvey. They are not a good example. They do not fit in at this school.'

'That —' Dinah had been going to say that it would be difficult. But just in time she remembered that he did not like argument. Better to be quiet and obey. Until she had had time to think everything over, to try and work out why the school was so strange. 'Yes sir,' she murmured.

As she went out and shut the door, her head was

humming with thoughts. Asleep? All the morning? It did not make sense. And had the Headmaster simply sat and stared at her all that time, without trying to wake her up? She shuddered and put a finger into her mouth to suck it thoughtfully.

Something made her take the finger out again and look at it. It was sore. There was a small red patch at one end, as if a pin had been driven into it. But she did not remember having pricked her finger. Frowning, she walked along the corridor towards the dining hall.

'The Best School I've Ever Been To'

*A*t the door of the dining hall, Dinah stopped. She
must be too early. There was no sound coming
from inside, none of the hubbub of chatter that she
associated with dinner time. But when she pushed the
door open she saw that the room was full. Table after
table of demure children in green uniforms eating platefuls
of sausages and chips. Going to the counter, she collected
a tray and looked round for Lloyd and Harvey.

It was easy to see them. Although the dining hall was
crowded, the table they sat at was half empty. The two
of them were sharing it with Ian and two girls, one tall
and red-haired and the other short and chubby. The

remaining five seats were vacant. Dinah walked across and sat down in one of them.

No one spoke to her. Harvey gave a shy smile, but Lloyd scowled and looked away and the others all stared at her, in a hostile way. Dinah chewed calmly for a moment before she said anything. Then she turned to Lloyd.

'I'm in your class.'

'Oh good,' Lloyd said sarcastically. 'Where've you been all the morning, then?'

'Went to see the Headmaster.' She finished off her first sausage.

Lloyd and Harvey exchanged glances and Ian looked at her curiously. 'What do you think of him?' he said.

Dinah opened her mouth to say that she thought he was creepy and peculiar. Instead, she heard her voice say, 'He is a marvellous man and this is the best school I've ever been to.' She put her knife and fork down.

'Ah ha!' said the chubby little girl savagely. The red-haired girl prodded her.

'Be quiet, Ingrid.'

'But Mandy —'

'Be quiet.'

The five of them went on eating stolidly, while Dinah studied their faces. But she could not guess anything from them. They were determinedly blank. After a moment or two, Mandy said casually, as if the question had not been asked already, 'What do you think of the Head-master?'

Automatically, Dinah found herself repeating the same

words. 'He is a marvellous man and this is the best school I've ever been to.'

'Ah *ha!*' said Ingrid again, unrepentantly. The others simply snorted and went on eating their dinner.

'But I don't understand.' Dinah looked round at them.

'They all say that.' Lloyd shrugged. 'All of *them*.' He waved a hand round at the rest of the dining hall. 'Try asking them some time. They think he's just as marvellous as you do. I can see you're going to fit in beautifully.'

Dinah looked over her shoulder at the green-uniformed children. Then she looked back at the hostile faces opposite her. She could not understand what was going on. She was not used to not understanding things. And she did not like it at all.

'I bet he said you were to go into the Hall after dinner,' Ingrid said sneeringly.

'Well, yes, he did. Doesn't everyone?'

'No,' Mandy said quietly. 'We don't. Everyone else does.'

Ian gave a languid, amused smile. '*We* have extra work. With one of the prefects to watch over us.'

'And you needn't go thinking we're thick or anything.' Lloyd slurped up the rest of his semolina, the noise sounding disastrously loud in the quiet canteen. 'It's not that at all. We just aren't like the others.'

'Oh,' said Dinah. She still did not understand anything, but she made up her mind not to say so. She would just watch and wait.

Lloyd got to his feet. 'Mind you're not late to the

Hall,' he said nastily. 'You don't want to get into trouble on your first day, do you?'

He turned away, and the others followed him. Harvey, going last, whispered 'Good luck,' and then hurried after, as if he were afraid the others might have heard him. As the five of them passed down the long canteen, two hundred pairs of eyes watched them expressionlessly, while two hundred sets of teeth chewed in rhythm.

Ten minutes later, as if at a signal, everyone stood up. As Dinah was beginning to expect, the children formed a neat crocodile, without any pushing, and began to file silently out of the canteen.

Waiting until nearly everyone had gone, Dinah found herself walking behind Lucy, the little girl who had not known the capital of the United States. She reached out and touched her on the arm. Lucy turned round with a jerk and then smiled timidly.

'Thank you,' she whispered. 'For what you did in the playground.'

''S all right.' Dinah smiled back. 'Can't think why the others wouldn't tell you.'

Lucy shrugged and started to turn away again, but Dinah had had an idea.

'Have you been at this school a long time?' she murmured.

'Since I was five,' Lucy whispered. 'Ssh! We're not supposed to talk.' She looked nervously over her shoulder.

'There's no one there,' Dinah said encouragingly. 'We're the last. Do you like the school?'

She had half expected the answer, but it was still a shock when she heard it. Lucy turned to look at her and said in a rather mechanical voice, 'The Headmaster is a marvellous man, and this is the best school I've ever been to.'

'It's the *only* school you've ever been to,' Dinah said.

But Lucy only looked puzzled and put her finger to her lips. Dinah walked on quietly, her thin face wrinkled with concentration. There was something very queer here. Something not like a school at all. Perhaps she would understand it better after she had seen what the Assembly in the Hall was like.

Following Lucy in, she sat down in a chair at the back of the Hall. It was full of children, and teachers were seated on chairs round the edge, as silent and stony-faced as their pupils. After a moment, the Headmaster appeared. He stalked up the aisle between the chairs, his long gown flapping behind him, seeming even taller than Dinah had remembered. Slowly he climbed the steps up to the stage and turned to look down on the crowded hall below him. There was no need for him to call for silence. Everyone, teachers and children alike, was gazing at him. With a thin smile, he reached up and took off his glasses and his huge green eyes stared out at them.

Dinah felt that he was looking directly at her. She could not move her eyes away from his steady green stare. Then he began to speak.

'Funny,' he said gently, 'that you should all be so tired. So early in the afternoon.'

But that's what he said before, Dinah thought, with a

jerk of surprise. *When I was in his office. It's peculiar.*

Her amazement had jolted her out of the dreamy vagueness that his voice was producing in the others. All of a sudden, she felt grimly stubborn. She had had enough peculiar happenings for one day. She tried to turn her attention away from the tall black figure on the stage, so that she could think. But it was very difficult. There seemed to be no escaping those eyes. Then, all at once, like a light, she had a little flicker of understanding.

That's it! She thought triumphantly. *When he takes his glasses off – when I see his eyes – I want to go to sleep. And that's when things get peculiar.*

With an almost gleeful feeling, she shut her own eyes tightly, blacking out the Hall, the rows of yawning children and the compelling green stare. This time she would not get caught.

'You all look very tired,' said the Headmaster's hissing voice.

No I don't, Dinah said rebelliously, inside her head, behind her closed eyes.

'*So* tired,' he went on. 'Your hands and feet are heavy, and your eyelids are like lead.'

No they're not, Dinah thought ferociously. She turned her head sideways and, with great caution, opened one eye. All around her, she could see heads starting to nod. Children were rubbing their eyes. Teachers were giving huge, uncontrollable yawns. Then, gradually, the eyelids closed. Dinah shut her own eyes again and listened.

'You are asleep,' the Headmaster hissed down the Hall.

Ha ha! No I'm not, Dinah's inside voice said rudely

and triumphantly. She was going to do it. She was going to get the better of him.

'When you wake up,' his voice went on silkily, 'you will remember that you saw a film about ants. If anyone asks, you will say, "It was a film about ants. It was very interesting. We saw how they build their nests and look after their eggs and how their queen lives." If you are asked any more questions, you will say, "I don't remember." Now, repeat that, please. What did you do in Assembly today?'

'It was a film about ants . . .' the children started, their voices wooden, in perfect unison. Dinah joined in, trying to sound as lifeless as the rest of them, but all the time she was gloating, because *she* knew that what she was saying was a lie. Even if she did not understand why she was supposed to be lying.

As the children stopped speaking, there was a pause and, unable to resist the urge, Dinah opened her eyes a fraction to glance at the rows and rows of apparently sleeping children, their faces turned to the front and their hands clasped in their lap. There was something sinister about the sight and, before she could stop herself, she shuddered. Instantly, she closed her eyes tightly and dropped her head forward, imitating theirs, but it was too late. From the front of the Hall she heard heavy footsteps coming down the aisle towards her.

'Dinah Glass, open your eyes,' said the Headmaster's voice softly.

Mechanically, she opened them, letting her gaze settle on a distant point, way past the Headmaster, hoping that he would think she was asleep. She could not see his face, but for a moment she thought that she had succeeded in deceiving him. He stood perfectly still, watching her.

Then she heard him say. 'Your left arm is completely numb. You can feel nothing.'

Oh yes I can, her mind said obstinately – a split second before she realized what he was going to do.

He leaned forward and she felt a sharp pain, darting into her left forearm. Unable to stop herself, she winced, looking down to see him pull out the pin with which he had pricked her.

'As I thought,' he said sharply. 'Pretending. Look at me, Dinah, when I'm speaking to you.'

She went on looking stubbornly at the floor.

'Look at me!' This time his voice was loud and threatening. Frightened in spite of herself, Dinah looked up.

He was staring straight at her, a lock of pale hair falling over his forehead and his green eyes wide and translucent.

'I can see that you are not yet accustomed to our ways,' he said, more quietly. 'I hope you are not going to be a person who won't cooperate with me.'

'It depends what you want,' Dinah said coldly.

'But it's not what *I* want.' He sounded almost amused. 'It's what *you* want.'

'What I want?'

'Yes,' he crooned. 'What you want. You want to go to sleep. Because you're so tired. So very, very tired.'

Too late, she realized that she had let herself get caught off guard. This time, try as she would, she could not close her eyes or turn them away from those great pools of green that seemed to swim closer and closer . . .

'You are so sleepy,' murmured the Headmaster. 'You feel you have to go to sleep . . .'

I'll forget it all, Dinah thought frantically. *I'll forget everything I've discovered. What a waste.*

As her eyelids began to droop, she gathered all her energies together, to try and fix something in her mind.

Remember it, remember it, hypnotism, hypnotism, HYPNOTISM. Grimly, she struggled to concentrate. *Remember it, remember it, hypnotism, hypno-, hyp- . . .*

But the words in her head drifted off into silence and floated away on a great tide of sleep as she slumped slowly forwards in her chair.

This time she did not feel a thing when the Headmaster stuck the pin into her arm.

CHAPTER 5

Assembly – Keep Out

Harvey looked up from his page of sums and stared out of the window, fidgeting. All around him, the others were working hard. Ian was writing steadily, in his elegant, sloping script, Mandy was frowning over a difficult problem, and Ingrid was running her hands through her untidy hair and chewing the end of her pencil. Even Lloyd was not paying him any attention. But Harvey could not concentrate. Because Dinah had made him think about Assembly again. What *did* go on in the Hall when they were all in here?

'Harvey!' said Rose sharply, looking up from the book she was reading. 'Why aren't you working?'

'I'm just thinking for a moment.' That was true enough, anyway. He waited until Rose was bent over her book again and then prodded Lloyd. 'What d'you think they're doing?' he mouthed noiselessly, pointing towards the Hall.

Lloyd frowned at him and mouthed back. 'Films, of course. Get on with your work.'

Harvey looked across at the Hall and frowned. The blackout curtains were certainly drawn, as if for a film. But all round the edges of the curtains he could see thin streaks of light. And it was always like that. Every day. He often looked across while he was supposed to be working, and he had never seen the lights go out. Not once. So they could not really be watching films. What *were* they doing? He wriggled in his chair with frustrated curiosity.

'Harvey Hunter, *will* you sit still and get on!' Rose was really irritated now. Harvey could see that he would have to be careful, or something nasty would happen. He was just about to go back to his sums when he suddenly had an idea.

'But I can't concentrate, Rose,' he said, making his voice into a whine. 'I want to go to the toilet.'

Rose looked even more annoyed. 'You should learn not to be so disorganized.'

'*Please*, Rose.' He knew he sounded stupid, but he could not bear it any longer. He *had* to go and have a look in the Hall. 'Please. I can't wait till the end of school.'

She looked rattled for a moment, as the prefects always

did when you asked them something unexpected. Then she nodded reluctantly. 'Oh, all right. But be as quick as you can.'

As he jumped up, he saw the others looking at him. Mandy's gentle face was worried. She had guessed he was up to something. He slipped quickly out of the door before she could mouth a question at him and ran along the corridor on tiptoe, until he reached the Hall doors.

The double doors had glass panels at the top, with heavy curtains drawn across. By stretching up and peering, he could see through a narrow gap at one side, and he stood there looking.

There was no screen on the stage, no projector, no sign at all of anyone getting ready to show a film. Instead, everyone in the Hall, teachers and children, were staring fixedly at the stage.

On the stage stood the Headmaster, stooped forward like a giant vulture. Harvey saw, with amazement, that he had taken off his dark glasses. *But I've never seen him like that*, Harvey thought. *Except on the first day I came here.* He leaned further forwards, pressing his nose against the glass in an effort to try and find out what was going on.

The Headmaster seemed to be reading aloud from a book that he held in his hands. As Harvey watched he stopped, then glanced up and spoke a few words. Immediately, all the people in the Hall started to chant in a regular monotone, as if they were repeating back, from memory, what he had read. It must have been pages long, because the voices went on and on and on. But, struggle as he might, Harvey could not make out more than a few words. He caught '. . . system . . .' several times and, once, a number '. . . minus twenty-six point nine . . .', but none of it made any sense. And still the voices went tirelessly on.

It was tempting to stay, to try to find out more, but just in time Harvey remembered that he would spoil his excuse if he did not get back quickly. Gnawing his bottom lip, he hurried away along the corridor.

He did not look back. If he had, he would have seen Jeff slide out from behind a tall bookcase beyond the Hall doors and stare after him with a gloating smile on his face. But it never occurred to him to glance over his shoulder. He was too busy getting back to the classroom.

As he let himself in, Rose scowled at him.

'You were too long.'

'Sorry.' He slid into his chair. Better write hard for a bit, until she had stopped watching him. He scratched away industriously, keeping an eye on her under his eyelids. When he was certain that she was deep in her book, he scrawled a message on a spare piece of paper.

They weren't watching films, so sucks. They were listening to the Headmaster.

With great care, he flicked it across on to Lloyd's desk. Lloyd gave him a disapproving frown, but when he had read the note he raised his eyebrows and a few moments later another note landed on Harvey's desk.

We'll ask Dinah when we get home.

★

As they sat over their tea, Dinah was even quieter than usual. She gazed into her cup, watching the brown liquid swirl round, and Mrs Hunter had to ask her three times whether she wanted another piece of cake.

'Sorry.' She looked up at last.

'Thinking about school?' Mrs Hunter smiled. 'I was going to ask if you had a nice day. What did you think of it?'

'I think,' Dinah said steadily, 'that the Headmaster is a marvellous man and this is the best school I've ever been to.'

Harvey sniffed scornfully and looked at Lloyd, but Lloyd was watching Dinah. Her face had gone white, almost as if she were frightened by what she had said. The next instant, she had lowered her eyes and began to munch her piece of cake.

'Let's all go in the playroom,' Lloyd said suddenly. 'Come on, H. You coming, Dinah?'

Dinah swallowed her mouthful of cake. 'If you like,' she said carefully.

She followed them through and sat down as Lloyd closed the door.

'Now,' he said, 'suppose you tell us what you were all doing in the Hall this afternoon.'

Dinah said mechanically, 'We saw a film.'

Lloyd looked knowingly at Harvey. 'Oh yes? What was it about?'

Dinah took a deep breath and began to talk as if she were reciting. 'It was a film about ants. It was very interesting. We saw how they build their nests and look after their eggs and how their queen lives.' She stopped abruptly.

'What else was it about?' Lloyd said.

'I don't remember.'

'Did the Headmaster talk to you about it afterwards?'

'I don't remember.'

'Rubber ravioli!' Lloyd burst out, 'don't you remember anything? You're a proper dunce, aren't you?'

Harvey giggled suddenly. 'She'll never be on Eddy Hair's Great School Quiz.'

'Oh, shut up about stupid Eddy Hair,' snapped Dinah. 'What's all this about, anyway?'

'Oh, nothing,' Lloyd said airily. 'We just wanted to know what happened, that's all. But if you're too thick to remember anything . . .'

'I *always* remember things,' Dinah said slowly. 'Always. I don't quite understand.' For a moment she looked as if she were going to go on. Then her face snapped shut and she shook her head. 'I've told you what I can. I can't tell you any more.'

'But I can tell you something,' Harvey said.

'Be quiet, you idiot.' Lloyd gave him a shove.

'No.' Harvey looked obstinate. 'It's not fair to ask her questions and then not tell her. Besides, I want to hear what she's got to say.' He turned back to Dinah. 'I sneaked out of our room and had a look through the Hall door. I didn't see any sign of a film.'

Dinah stared at him and he nodded.

'That's right. Nothing. No screen or projector or anything. And I was watching from across the playground all the rest of the time. The lights in the Hall didn't go out once. So you can't have seen a film. You're lying.'

'What did you see?' Dinah said hesitantly.

'I saw you all sitting looking at the Headmaster on the stage. He read something long out of a book and you all repeated it back. I don't know what it was, but you must know. You all said it from memory.'

Dinah frowned harder and shook her head. 'I don't remember anything like that happening.'

'Huh!' Lloyd sat down and stretched his legs out. 'What did happen then?'

'I told you. We saw a film. It was a film about ants.' She was talking in that steady, reciting voice again. 'It was very interesting. We saw how they build their nests and look after their eggs and how their queen lives.'

'That's what you said before.' Harvey bounced up. 'It's *exactly* what you said before.'

'And it's not true.' Lloyd banged his hand down on the table. 'So why do you keep saying it?'

'I – I don't know.' For a moment, Dinah looked bewildered. Then her face pinched. 'I don't want to talk about it. Why do you keep going on about it?'

'Because it's ridiculous,' Lloyd snapped. 'You heard what Harvey saw.'

Dinah was beginning to look annoyed. A faint pink flush ran along her cheekbones, and the tip of her nose turned white.

'You hadn't got any business to be seeing anything,' she said crossly. 'What did you think you were doing, snooping around like that?'

'I thought there was something peculiar going on,' Harvey said mildly. 'And I was right, wasn't I?'

'You don't know anything about it,' Dinah muttered. 'And if you go on nosing, you'll get into trouble.'

'I told you not to tell her anything, H!' Lloyd burst out. 'Bright green baked beans! Suppose she goes off and tells the Headmaster what you said?'

Harvey turned pale. 'Oh, but she wouldn't do that. Would you, Di?'

'Of course not,' Dinah started to say. Then she stopped and looked craftily at Lloyd. 'At least, I might be tempted to. If you don't leave me alone.'

'Don't you dare!' Lloyd jumped to his feet. 'Harvey hasn't done anything wrong.'

'Oh no?' Dinah said triumphantly. 'Then why is he looking so scared?'

She was right. Harvey's round face had crumpled with fright, and he was twitching nervously at the edge of his jumper.

'He was silly, that's all,' Lloyd said. 'I've told him a hundred times not to get involved with things. But he didn't do anything *wrong.*'

'Can't he speak for himself?' Dinah said scornfully. 'Look at him. He's shaking like a jelly. He's nothing but a baby. Running round the school and peering in at windows. It's so childish.'

'That's all you know.' Lloyd had gone red in the face. 'It was a silly thing to do, but it was very brave. Only I don't suppose you would understand.'

'Why not?' Suddenly, Dinah went very quiet. She

41

stopped looking at Lloyd and turned to Harvey. 'Why don't you explain to me? I know *he* doesn't like me –' she waved a hand towards Lloyd '– but you've been quite nice really. And I want to understand. Why was it so brave of you to look in at the Hall?'

'Don't tell her a thing,' Lloyd said sharply.

'Go on,' Dinah said in a soft voice. 'Tell me, Harvey. What's going on in that school? Why is everyone so well behaved? And what do you think happens in Assembly?'

'I – I don't know,' Harvey stuttered, 'but –'

Suddenly, Lloyd darted at Dinah, pushing her through the door and into the hall, with one gigantic shove. Slamming the door shut, he leaned against it and glared at Harvey.

'Haven't you got any sense at all, H? Can't you get it into your thick head that she's one of them? If you tell her anything – anything at all – she'll probably go off and repeat it all to the Headmaster. And then you'll get me and all the others into trouble as well.'

Harvey went even paler. 'I don't think she would. Not really. Would she?'

'I don't know,' Lloyd said grimly. 'We'll just have to wait and see, won't we?'

Harvey chewed nervously at the end of his finger.

From outside in the hall came the sound of voices. Mr Hunter had come in and he was saying to Dinah, 'How did you get on at school, then? What do you think of it?'

Dinah's mechanical voice came clearly through the door.

'I think the Headmaster is a marvellous man and this is the best school I've ever been to.'

CHAPTER 6

Snow

Dinah sat up in bed for a long time that night, a stiff little figure in a white nightdress, hugging her knees. She knew that there was something wrong about the school, with its well-behaved children, all doing the right thing at the right moment, but she could not understand what it was. And she knew that she did not like the Headmaster at all. She could not understand why she kept saying how wonderful he was. She hated not understanding things.

In the end, she did what she always did when things baffled her. Slipping quietly out of bed, she pulled back the curtains so that the room was lit by moonlight from outside. Then she went to stand in front of the mirror. Pale and prim, her reflection stared back at her, the eyes thoughtful and the mouth pursed up, considering.

'Well?' she murmured. 'What's wrong? Why is the school so peculiar?'

Gazing into her own eyes, she suddenly knew the answer. *Fear. It's because they're all afraid.*

She nodded briskly. Yes, that was the right answer. 'But what are they afraid of?'

The reflection stared back, unwinking, and she heard the reply in her head. *That's what you'll have to find out.*

'How?' But she hardly needed to ask. The answer to that one was obvious.

You'll have to be naughty, and see what happens to you.

Her hands, clasped on top of the dressing table, began to shake slightly, but the face that looked back at her out of the mirror was amused.

See? You're afraid yourself, and you don't know why.

Defiantly, she stuck her chin up and pulled a face into the mirror. 'I don't care if I am scared,' she said out loud. 'I want to know, and if that's the only way to find out, that's what I'll do.'

With a determined hand, she closed the curtains and climbed back into bed, feeling as though she had settled something. Curling up under the covers, she fell asleep trying to think of something bad she could do.

When the morning came, she was still considering. She did not expect Lloyd and Harvey to speak to her after their quarrel the day before, and she came down to breakfast in a proud silence, not saying anything even to Mrs Hunter. But things were a bit different. Something had happened that she had not counted on.

It had finally snowed. Outside in the garden, a white, unbroken sheet stretched across the grass, gleaming in the crisp, clear light. And Harvey was so excited that he had forgotten about everything else. He wriggled delightedly in his chair.

'Oh, I *wish* we didn't have to go to school today. Don't you, Di?'

'Sky-blue sandwiches!' snorted Lloyd, his mouth full of porridge, 'd'you ever want to go to school?'

'No, but it's different today,' Harvey said earnestly. 'If we stayed at home, we could build a snowman and have a snowball fight and – oh, Mum, couldn't we?'

'Don't be silly, dear,' Mrs Hunter said placidly. 'There's no point in asking questions like that. Just make sure you wrap up warmly. You know the cold's bad for your chest.'

She hovered over them while they dressed, insisting on bundling Harvey up in extra scarves and gloves, until he looked like a little round parcel. And all the time he was hopping up and down, peering longingly out of the window at the snow. When she finally let them go, Harvey ran joyfully outside and kicked his boots about, scattering a fine dust of snow.

'Oh, it's beautiful! It's lovely! Don't you think it's gorgeous, Di?'

'Yes, I like snow,' she said dreamily. 'We used to have terrific snowball fights at the Children's Home. The sort where you pick sides and build up great stocks of snowballs before you start.'

'Oh, fantastic!' Harvey reached down for a handful of snow.

'Come on!' Lloyd said crossly. 'We'll be late for school.'

Harvey's face drooped. Still deep in her own thoughts, Dinah said, 'We could always have a snowball fight in the playground. In morning playtime.'

She was so busy thinking of her own plans for the day that she did not notice how Harvey brightened and started to whistle. All she could think of was that she had found a good way to be naughty.

She was so busy thinking, in fact, that she walked into school and into her classroom in a daze. It was not until she was sitting in her desk that she realized that she had automatically moved into line and marched in with the others, as if she had been told what to do. But she did not remember anyone having told her.

Before she had time to work that one out, however, she had another surprise. Mr Venables, the class teacher, was giving out pieces of paper.

'This morning,' he said, as he moved round the room, 'I want you to write down everything you know about the solar system.'

As it happened, Dinah knew a great deal about the solar system. But she had no intention of writing it all down. That would be asking for trouble. She settled down to consider what she could safely say. But before she had thought about it at all, she found herself writing, in strange, stiff little sentences.

'The planets of the solar system are Mercury, Venus, Earth, Mars, Jupiter, Saturn, Uranus, Neptune and Pluto.

The sun is the star of the solar system.

The Earth is 0.137 light-hours from the sun.

The magnitude of the sun is − 29.6.'

She stopped, with an effort, and stared at the last sentence she had written. *But I didn't know that*, she thought. She never remembered seeing that particular piece of information before. Yet there it was, confidently written down on her piece of paper, as though someone had slipped it into her head without her knowing.

Cautiously, she leaned sideways, to glance at the paper on the desk next to her. The boy beside her had just written, 'The magnitude of the sun is − 29.6.'

Although the classroom was warm, she found herself shivering. Everyone in the room was scribbling busily, and she was suddenly sure that they had all just written, 'The magnitude of the sun is − 29.6.' Thirty little robots, all obediently writing down the same things, things that had been put into their heads for them. The only person who was not writing was Lloyd. He was chewing the end of his pencil, as if he did not know very much about the solar system. Dinah let herself feel a little quiver of mean pleasure that he was in trouble. Then she started to write again, and the information went on pouring out. Most of it she knew, but every now and again came a little bit she did not.

And as she wrote, she pursed her lips together determinedly. Things were getting queerer and queerer. And she would find out why. She *would*.

At playtime, she put on her hat and coat and marched out into the playground, ready to carry out her plan. Without speaking to anyone, she knelt down and began to make a heap of snowballs, intending to throw them when she had a pile of ten.

But she had reckoned without Harvey. When she was only halfway through, he came bounding across to her, past all the groups of children chanting tables and dates.

'Oh Di! You remembered!'

'What?' She looked up, vaguely.

'You remembered. We really *are* going to have a snowball fight!'

Suddenly she realized what she had done. 'No. Harvey! I didn't mean you.'

'Don't be a spoilsport.' He bent down and picked up two of the snowballs she had made.

Almost at once, Lloyd was there. He came bounding across the playground at top speed. 'H! What are you doing?'

'We're going to have a snowball fight,' Harvey said cheerfully. 'It's Di's idea.'

'Don't be an idiot.' Lloyd knocked the snowballs out of his hands. 'Let her get into trouble if she wants to, but don't you get mixed up with it.'

'That's right,' Dinah said. She did not realize how odd it sounded until she saw Lloyd staring at her. She stared back defiantly, and while the two of them were distracted,

Harvey stooped down and picked up two more snowballs.

'I think you're both rotten!' he shouted. 'And I *will* have a snowball fight. The snow might be all gone, by tomorrow.'

His yell sounded eerily loud among the mutters in the playground. As he drew his right arm back to throw, Lloyd shouted warningly, 'H! No!' And from the other side of the playground came the sound of Ian's voice, calling, 'Watch out, you lot!'

But it was too late. As total silence fell over the playground, the two snowballs flew from Harvey's gloved hands and spattered messily, one on Lloyd's coat and one on Dinah's.

'Lloyd and Harvey Hunter! Dinah Glass! Come here!' bellowed a voice from the steps.

Ranged on the steps, the prefects were staring at them, a row of six stern faces. Slowly, Lloyd, Harvey and Dinah walked to the foot of the steps and stood looking up.

'Wait there!' Rose said curtly. 'We'll deal with you when the others have gone inside.'

CHAPTER 7

The Punishment

As Rose began to call out orders, the neat rows of children formed and filed into the building. Lloyd, Harvey and Dinah stood awkwardly, not looking at each other, until the whole playground was empty and they were alone, gazing up at the prefects, who stood like a row of iron statues.

Jeff stared down at them and chanted, 'It is forbidden to waste time by playing in the playground.'

'It is forbidden,' Rose went on, 'to make a mess of your school uniform.'

'You must be punished,' Sarah said.

'In a suitable manner,' finished off Simon, smiling slightly.

Drawing together, the prefects whispered for a moment and then Rose turned to them again. 'Go inside,' she rapped out. 'Take off your hats and coats and gloves. Then come back here.'

As they walked towards the cloakroom, Dinah whispered to Lloyd, 'What will happen? What will they do?'

'I don't know,' he said sourly. 'But whatever it is, it'll be all your fault. I wish you'd never come.'

'No, it's my fault,' Harvey said in a miserable voice. 'I threw the snowballs. And whatever they do, it'll be *terrible*.'

When they came out of the door again, four of the prefects had gone. Rose was standing looking out over the playground, with a pleased smile on her face, and Jeff was by her side, holding three long-handled brooms.

'Now,' he said in a silky voice, 'you're very lucky. We've decided to be kind to you.'

Lloyd and Harvey looked uneasily at each other.

'Yes.' Rose's smile broadened. 'Because you're so fond of playing with the snow, we're going to let you have some more of it.'

Jeff held out the brooms. 'You will each take one of these, and you will sweep all the snow from the playground into a heap. Then,' he looked at Rose, with a grin, 'you will make the whole heap into a pile of snowballs.'

For a second, Harvey looked perplexed, but Lloyd burst out, 'Aren't you going to let us put on our coats and things?'

Rose went on smiling. 'Certainly not.'

'But you can't do that! Harvey's got a weak chest. He could be ill. He –'

'Silence!'

'Suppose we say no?' asked Dinah, in a stiff voice.

Rose and Jeff looked at her as if she had said something unbelievably stupid. Together, they chanted, 'The prefects are the voice of the Headmaster. They must be obeyed.'

Then Jeff thrust the brooms at them. 'Get sweeping!'

Resigned, Lloyd and Harvey trailed off down the steps, dragging their brooms after them. Dinah lingered rebelliously for a second or two, then joined them at the far end of the playground.

'Let's do it as quickly as we can,' she said. 'Perhaps that'll keep us warm.'

'Huh!' Lloyd snorted. 'Don't know why you're so cheerful. None of this would have happened if you hadn't started talking about snowball fights.'

He banged his broom crossly into the snow and began to sweep, pushing it into a great white mound in front of him.

For the first ten minutes or so, it was not too bad. The exercise kept them fairly warm. But then the wind started to blow, scattering the snow as they swept it and freezing their fingers.

'I'm so cold,' Harvey said plaintively. 'And we're only halfway across. We'll never get it all swept.'

'Don't give up yet,' Lloyd said grimly. 'This is the easy part. Just you wait until we start on the snowballs.'

Dinah shuddered at the thought, as the wind whipped through her thin school shirt. Then she found that she could not stop shivering. Her whole body was shaking, and her teeth were clattering together uncontrollably. She put down her broom for a moment to clap her arms round herself, for a bit of warmth.

Instantly, from the building behind them, came an irate rapping. Turning, she saw Rose gesturing furiously at her through the window. She picked up her broom again and began to sweep harder, trying to ignore the shaking.

At last the snow was piled into a single heap, almost as tall as Harvey. The three of them laid their brooms down at one side and stared at it.

'I don't think I can do it,' Harvey said woefully. 'My hands are *hurting*.'

Lloyd watched him anxiously. His face had a bluish tinge and he was starting to breathe wheezily.

'Why don't you stop?' Dinah said. 'Tell them you won't do it. I don't suppose the Headmaster would really be angry. He must see —' Then her teeth rattled together so hard that she could not go on speaking.

Lloyd and Harvey said nothing. Just looked at her as though she were completely idiotic and bent down to start making snowballs.

'Oh, all right,' she said crossly. 'Be like that. I bet I can make snowballs faster than you.'

As soon as she touched the snow, she knew that it was going to be a nightmare. Her hands were already painfully cold, but at least they had been dry up to now. The snow made them wet, and the cold wind, whipping across, stung them so that they felt almost as if they were burning. Anxiously, she wondered how long it would take before she got frostbite and her fingers started to turn black and drop off.

It would not have been quite so bad if Lloyd and Harvey had been sympathetic, but neither of them spoke to her. Lloyd was making snowballs in a frenzy, trying to get through the huge heap as quickly as possible. If he looked at her at all, it was only to pull a disgusted face. And Harvey had started to cry. Without stopping work, he was sobbing with pain, his face growing red and raw now as the wind scoured the tears from his round cheeks.

I can't, murmured a voice in Dinah's head. *I can't, I can't, I can't*. But all the time, mechanically, she went on making snowballs, until it seemed that she would never stop, as if she would go on until the end of the world, stooping, seizing a handful of snow, squashing it together in her agonized hands and dropping it on to the pile.

They seemed to have been there for about a hundred years when Lloyd said suddenly, 'Two or three more each and we've finished.' Glancing sideways at his watch, Dinah saw that it was not yet twelve o'clock. Gritting her teeth, she scrunched together the last couple of handfuls of snow and flung them triumphantly on top of the pile.

'That's it. We've finished! Let's go inside and get warm.'

'Not yet,' Lloyd said bitterly. 'Look. They're coming to inspect us.'

Sure enough, the prefects, all six of them, were trooping down the steps from the school, marching in perfect time. They walked across the playground and stood in a half-circle round Lloyd, Harvey and Dinah.

'Not a very tidy heap of snowballs,' Rose said grudgingly. She looked sideways at Jeff, and his spotty face suddenly creased into a leering smile.

'But you must have enjoyed yourselves,' he said softly. 'Since you're so *fond* of snow. Do you think they've had enough snow yet, Rose?'

She leered back at him. 'Surely not. Not when they like it so much.'

Without warning, the line of prefects surged forwards, in unison, their hands outstretched. Lloyd, Harvey and Dinah were each seized by two prefects who spun them round and knocked them forwards, face down in the snow.

As Dinah's face crashed down into the hard, balled snow, her first feeling was one of despair. Snow slammed up her nose, into her eyes and all down her front, soaking her clothes. It seemed like the last straw, and she nearly burst into tears. But by the time she stood up, she was furious. Furious and incredulous. Leaping to her feet, she began to yell at the prefects.

'That's too much! You can't do that! I shall go and tell the Headmaster. He'll punish you. You've got no right to treat us like that.'

Very softly, Jeff started to laugh and Rose, shaking

with merriment, pointed a finger towards the school,
where the window of the Headmaster's office faced
them.

At the window was a pale face, its eyes hidden behind
dark glasses. It stared out over the playground, apparently
without expression.

'So he knows, does he?' Dinah said quietly. Her mouth
set stubbornly. 'Well, I'm not scared of him, even if the
rest of you are. I shall go and tell him just what I think
of him for letting something like this happen to a boy as
little as Harvey.'

Her feet sounding loud on the cleared tarmac, she
stamped across the playground and into the school, carried
along by the force of her cold rage. Without stopping to
consider what she was doing, she marched up to the door
of the Headmaster's office and hammered on it with both
fists.

Nothing happened.

Crossly, she caught at the handle and rattled it, but the
door was locked, and so heavy that it hardly moved.

'I know you're in there!' she shouted. 'I saw you at
the window. And I think it's disgusting. Fancy letting
the prefects bully a little boy like Harvey. It might make
him *ill*. You're inhuman.'

She paused. No sound came from behind the door
and, for a second, she felt completely helpless. Then, at
last, her brain began to work. She smiled triumphantly,
and went on speaking in a quieter voice.

'Anyway, you won't get away with this. Even Head-
masters aren't allowed to do things like that. When we

get home, we'll all tell Mr and Mrs Hunter, and there'll be a scandal. You'll be prosecuted.'

There was still no sound, but she did not care now that she had worked out what to do next. Her fingers were starting to hurt as the warmth of the building reached them, so, with a final thump on the door, she began to run down the corridor, towards the cloakrooms. If only she could wash them in warm water, she would feel better. And if there was something hot for lunch, even Harvey might be all right.

She was making so much noise, that she did not hear the office door open behind her. She did not look over her shoulder and see the pale face which stared after her. If she had, she would have been puzzled. Because the face was smiling.

'So, Miss Clever Glass,' murmured the Headmaster, 'you have a soft spot for Harvey Hunter, have you? You're ready to protect him? Well, that might come in very useful. Yes, indeed. I must think about that.' His smile broadened. 'After this afternoon's Assembly.' And as he turned away, he laughed, softly and evilly.

Lloyd burst in through the back door of the kitchen, a hundred yards ahead of Harvey and Dinah. 'Mum! Mum! Where are you?'

Mrs Hunter emerged from the hall. 'Goodness me, what a fuss. The end of the world at least, I should think. Whatever is the matter?'

'It's what happened at school today.' Lloyd slumped down into a chair. 'It was simply terrible.'

Mrs Hunter suddenly stopped looking sympathetic. 'Now, Lloyd, I hope this isn't going to be another one of your silly stories. You know what trouble we've had in the past, with your lies.'

'It's different this time,' Lloyd said triumphantly. 'Dinah will tell you that it's true. And you'll believe her, won't you?' He turned round and waved a hand at Harvey and Dinah, who were coming through the door.

'Well, Dinah certainly looks calmer than you do,' Mrs Hunter said.

'But she knows too,' Lloyd yelled. 'She'll tell you.'

'Don't shout, dear.'

'Oh, why don't you *ask* her?'

'Yes,' said Harvey excitedly. 'Ask Dinah what happened at school today.'

'You'll believe *her*,' Lloyd said bitterly.

Dinah was frowning, looking at the three of them in bewilderment.

'Well, dear?' Mrs Hunter said gently. 'Tell me. What happened at school today?'

In a perfectly calm, even voice. Dinah said. 'At school this morning. Harvey made snowballs and we all had a snowball fight. It was super. The Headmaster made sure we all dressed up warmly in our hats and coats and gloves. And he gave us drinks of hot blackcurrant when we came inside.'

'*What*?' Lloyd stared at her.

Harvey looked appalled. '*Dinah*!'

Mrs Hunter smiled comfortably. 'It all sounds very nice.'

'But you don't understand!' Lloyd exploded. 'It's not true. It wasn't like that at all. We –'

'Be quiet!' All at once, Mrs Hunter was very angry. 'It's always the same, Lloyd. You and Harvey come back from school with silly, unbelievable stories and whenever I ask any of the other children I find it's all lies. I'm *not* going to make a fool of myself by complaining again. I don't think it's funny, even if you do.'

'It's not *meant* to be funny!' Lloyd glared at Dinah. 'She knows that. She's a filthy, foul traitor! *She's* the one who's telling lies, and –'

'That's enough!' Mrs Hunter banged her hand on the table. 'I don't blame Dinah for not wanting to join in with your silly games. You've been unpleasant to her ever since she came, I won't have it. This is her home now, as well as yours, and you'll just have to get used to it.'

'But –'

'Not another word!'

'It doesn't matter, L,' Harvey said miserably. 'We ought to have known it would be like this. It's always like this. Two hundred people to say we're lying, whatever we say. We can't do anything about it.'

'We can refuse to speak to traitors,' Lloyd said hotly. 'Come on, H. Let's go to the playroom. There's a bad smell in this kitchen.'

He stamped out. Harvey stood in the doorway for a moment, looking at Dinah.

'How *could* you?' he said reproachfully. 'When you know what it was like?'

CHAPTER 8

Prefects' Meeting

'We won't speak to her,' Lloyd said. 'Not ever again. Understand, H?' He pulled on his sock with such ferocity that his big toe came through the end. With a shout of rage, he flung the sock into the wastepaper basket and took a clean one out of the drawer.

'But how can we not?' Harvey said miserably. 'She doesn't know anyone except us. If *we* don't talk to her —'

'Black bananas! Think I care about that? After the way she's treated us? You're too soft, H, that's what's wrong with you. Well, just watch it. If I catch you speaking to her, I won't look after you any more. And I'll tell the others not to look after you, either. Then you'll be in trouble.' Ramming his shoes on, Lloyd stamped off downstairs and a moment later an unhappy Harvey followed him.

They sat hunched over their plates of porridge, turned away from Dinah and talking only to each other. From time to time, Lloyd glanced at her, to see what effect they were having, but it was impossible to tell. She went on eating her breakfast without speaking, her cold, pale face gazing off into the distance.

When the time came to leave, she followed them out into the hall and left the house with them, but they marched along the road ten yards ahead of her, not looking over their shoulders.

'Just let her *dare* try to catch us up!' Lloyd muttered.

'She won't do that,' Harvey said. 'She's too proud. She –'

'Oh shut up! I don't want you going on about her all day. She's not here. She doesn't exist. Understand?'

Lloyd strode faster up the road and swept into the playground, his eyes searching about. 'We must find Ian and Mandy and Ingrid and warn them about her. Tell them not to talk to her either. Then she'll only have the goody-goodies and she won't get much fun out of them.'

He saw the other three in a corner and marched across to them, followed by Harvey. But before he could say anything, silence fell over the playground and everyone turned to look at the prefects.

There seemed to be something odd about them today. They were smirking at each other and hunting round the playground with their eyes, as if they were looking for somebody. Suddenly Ian poked Lloyd in the ribs.

'Hey,' he mouthed soundlessly, 'why are they all look-ing at Harvey?' It was true. Six pairs of eyes had fixed on Harvey's chubby figure and six smiles had grown wider. Harvey started to shake. Mandy reached out and gripped his hand comfortingly. 'Don't worry,' she mouthed. 'It might not be as bad as you think.'

But Harvey was already worried. As the prefects rapped out their orders and the children started to move into lines, he caught at Lloyd's sleeve. 'Don't leave me alone, L.'

'O K.' Lloyd patted his shoulder. 'We'll stick together.'

As they moved across the playground, he avoided his usual place and went to stand in Harvey's line instead, immediately behind him. He saw Dinah glance quickly across at him, but he ignored her.

'Lead – in!' Jeff shouted.

As the lines began to move, Lloyd put a steadying hand on Harvey's arm and the two of them walked together up the steps. When they were nearly at the top, Rose stuck out a hand, blocking Harvey's way.

'Harvey Hunter,' she intoned, 'you are summoned to appear before the Prefects' Council at ten o'clock.'

'Why?' Harvey said plaintively. 'I haven't done anything.'

'That's right,' Lloyd blustered. 'Leave him alone.'

Rose gave him an icy stare. 'You are in the wrong line, Lloyd Hunter.'

'That's because I'm sticking by Harvey. I don't know

what you're plotting, but I'm coming too.' He saw Rose open her mouth to protest and he said quickly, 'Even in the courts, people are allowed to have lawyers to speak for them.'

Rather to his surprise, Rose shrugged. 'Please yourself. You can be Harvey's lawyer. It won't do any good. Ten o'clock.'

For an hour, Lloyd sat in his classroom, chewing the end of his pencil. All around him, people were scribbling industriously, writing facts about the British Constitution. Lloyd did not know the facts – as usual – but this morning he did not even care. All he could think of was the minute hand on the clock on the wall. It seemed to be racing round towards ten o'clock at twice its normal speed.

At five to ten, he stuck his hand up.

'Yes?' barked Mr Venables, looking startled. People hardly ever put their hands up. It was not encouraged.

'Please, sir, I've got to go to the Prefects' Council.'

Mr Venables frowned. 'I was not informed. This is most disorderly.'

'I've got to go,' Lloyd insisted. Without even waiting for an answer, he bounded out of his seat and made for the door. He could see Dinah watching him and he almost pulled a face at her. Then he remembered. No communication.

Outside the door of the prefects' room, Harvey was standing shivering. 'Oh, what do you think is going on? What are they going to do to me now?'

'Dunno. We'll have to go in and find out.' Lloyd slapped him encouragingly on the back. 'Cheer up. At least the snow's melted. They can't make us do that again, anyway.'

Boldly he hammered on the door and heard Jeff's voice say, 'Come in.'

The prefects were sitting in a line behind a long table, their faces grave and their uniforms immaculate. Each of them had a pen clipped neatly into the top blazer pocket, at precisely the same angle, and their hands were folded on the table in front of them in a straight row. Six doubled fists.

'Sit down,' said Rose, pointing at two chairs, drawn up on the other side of the table.

'What's this all about?' Lloyd muttered. 'What's going on?'

'Sit down!' Rose said again, more curtly. 'And don't speak unless we ask you questions.'

Lloyd and Harvey took the two chairs and sat facing the row of accusing eyes. Slowly, Jeff reached out for a grey folder which lay on the table. A neat label on the front said *Harvey Hunter*. Opening it, he pulled out a piece of paper.

'Harvey Hunter,' he began, 'we have called you before us, on the instructions of the Headmaster, to deal with your disobedient and disorderly behaviour this week. He has been most displeased with you.'

Rose nodded. 'You are a disruptive influence in the school.'

'That's nonsense,' Lloyd burst out. 'He's never influenced anybody.'

'Please be quiet,' said Jeff, 'and listen to the charges.'

He looked down at the piece of paper. 'You are accused of three things. First, on Monday, you came into school before you were called in by us, although you know it's against the rules to come in early. Have you anything to say?'

'I was going to do the registers,' Harvey faltered. 'The Headmaster told me to.'

Jeff shook his head and ran a finger down the paper. 'Clearly rubbish. My information is that Sharon Mandeville did the registers on Monday.'

'It was a mistake,' Lloyd said quietly. 'The Headmaster changed his mind.'

'The Headmaster never changes his mind,' Rose said crushingly. 'Indecision is disorder.'

'Second,' Jeff went on relentlessly, 'later the same day, in the afternoon, you left your classroom, telling Rose that you wanted to go to the toilet. Instead, you went up to the Hall, to spy on the Assembly – which you are not permitted to attend.'

Harvey gasped and turned to look at Lloyd, but this time Lloyd could only shrug.

'Third,' Jeff said, 'yesterday, in the playground, you threw two snowballs, although you knew that playing anywhere on school premises is most strictly forbidden.'

'But that's not fair!' Lloyd shouted. 'He's already been punished for that.'

'The prefects took such action as they saw fit,' Rose said crushingly, 'but the matter has not yet been dealt with by the Headmaster. We are now acting under his instructions.'

'I don't believe you,' Lloyd said. 'If the Headmaster wants to deal with Harvey, why doesn't he see him himself?'

But even as he spoke the words, he knew they were stupid. Simultaneously, the figures round the table chanted, 'The prefects are the voice of the Headmaster. They must be obeyed.'

'Well,' said Lloyd desperately, 'if you're the voice of the Headmaster, then when you punished Harvey yesterday, that *was* a punishment from the Headmaster. And it *isn't* fair to give him another one.'

Harvey twisted his hands together wretchedly. 'Oh, L, what's the use? This isn't really like a court. They're not going to let me off whatever you say. Why don't we just shut up and hear what they're going to do to me?'

Rose gave a patronizing smile. 'I'm glad to see that one of you has some sense. Especially since the Headmaster has decided to be merciful.'

'He has?' Harvey looked disbelieving.

Rose nodded. 'He will give you a chance to redeem yourself.' She reached into the file and drew out a long white envelope with Harvey's name written on the front. 'He has set you a paper of sums to do. If you get them all right, your offences will be forgotten. This time. But if you get any of them wrong, the Headmaster will deal with you himself. Most severely.'

Harvey gulped. 'Is that all? Can I go?'

Jeff nodded. 'Go straight back to your classrooms and get on with your work. The sums are not to be done until you get home.' He smiled sarcastically. 'You never know. If you do them well enough, you might land up on Eddy Hair's Great School Quiz.'

Lloyd snorted. 'I can just see *us* being the Headmaster's blue-eyed boys.'

Ignoring Jeff's frown, he made for the door. As soon as he and Harvey were safely outside, he exploded.

'Of all the stupid, trumped-up, unfair charges –'

Harvey looked sideways at him, his eyes scared. 'But how did they *know*, L? About me going into school early and going to look at the Assembly? No one knew about both things. Only me and you.'

Lloyd stopped in the middle of the corridor. 'Yes,' he said softly. 'Exploding eggshells! There *was* someone else who knew. Dinah saw you go into school early. And you told her that you watched the Assembly.'

'But she wouldn't have told. Would she?'

Lloyd pulled a face. 'Of course she would. It's all her fault you're in trouble. Like yesterday. That was her fault too.' Then he saw Harvey start to look upset and he put an arm round his shoulders. 'Never mind. It could be worse. They've only given you sums to do. And you're quite good at sums.'

'I expect they're hard,' Harvey faltered.

'Let's have a look.'

Harvey ripped open the envelope and pulled out three sheets of paper folded together. He glanced at them briefly and then said, in a horrified voice, 'L, I'll never work out the answers. I can't even understand the questions.'

'Let me see.' Lloyd snatched the papers out of his hand. 'I can always help you.'

He began to read with scornful confidence, but a moment later he, too, was looking completely baffled.

'You see?' Harvey said. 'We can't. Oh, what am I going to *do*?'

Lloyd took the envelope and pushed the papers back into it. 'We'll let Mandy have a look. She's quite good at sums. And if that doesn't work, we'll show them to Mum when we get home. She'll help you if she can. And if she can't –' all at once he looked pleased '– she'll see they're much too difficult for you. Then even she will have to admit there's something peculiar going on.'

When they got home, Mrs Hunter was sitting in the kitchen having a cup of tea with Dinah. Lloyd walked straight past Dinah without even looking at her.

'Mum, we want to talk to you.'

'Well, of course.' Mrs Hunter smiled. 'Have a cup of tea?'

Lloyd flicked his fingers impatiently. 'No. We want to talk to you alone.'

At once, his mother stiffened. 'I've told you about that before. Dinah's a member of the family and you must treat her like one. If you've got anything to say, you can say it with her here.'

'But you don't understand –' Lloyd began sulkily.

'Please, L,' Harvey broke in, 'don't waste time. Let's just show her the sums.' He pulled the papers out of the envelope and threw them on the table.

'The Headmaster gave them to him,' Lloyd said, 'and they're terrible. You must help him.'

Mrs Hunter shook her head. 'Now, you know you mustn't cheat. If the Headmaster gave them to Harvey, he means him to do them by himself.'

'But Mum, I can't,' Harvey said pathetically. 'They're awful. You look.'

Mrs Hunter picked up the paper and scanned it. Then she gave a little laugh. 'It's no use. It doesn't mean anything to me. I don't understand any of this New Maths you all do.'

'It's not New Maths!' Harvey shouted. 'It's just incredibly difficult.'

'Now, now, dear,' Mrs Hunter said, a little sharply, 'calm down. Let me give you a cup of tea. Then you can go away quietly by yourself and look at it. I'm sure you'll find it's all right when you think about it. The Headmaster wouldn't be unreasonable.'

'That's what you think,' Lloyd said bitterly. 'He's a maniac.'

'Don't be silly,' Mrs Hunter said. 'I'm sure he's not a maniac. Is he, Dinah?'

With an expression of utter misery on her face, Dinah said, 'The Headmaster is a marvellous man, and this is the best school I've ever been to.'

'It's no good asking *her*!' Lloyd shouted. 'It's all her fault. She's the one who got Harvey into trouble.'

'Me?' Dinah said.

'Yes, you!' He glared at her, and she stared back, looking completely baffled.

'Oh, what's the use of quarrelling?' Harvey said desperately. 'What does it matter? All that matters is that I've got these sums to do and *I can't do them*. And nobody can help me. It's going to be *awful*.' He snatched up the papers and ran out of the room, banging the door behind him.

'See what you've done?' Lloyd shouted at Dinah. 'Oh, I wish you'd never come!'

He ran after Harvey, banging the door again, and found him in the playroom, huddled in a chair. His shoulders were shaking and he was beginning to sob fiercely.

'Oh H, do stop it. That won't help.'

'Nothing will help,' said Harvey, in a totally wretched voice. 'I shan't be able to do the sums and tomorrow I'll have to go and see the Headmaster, and it will be frightful and – oh!' With a loud wail, he buried himself deep in the cushions.

At that moment, the playroom door opened again.

'Please may I see the sums?' said a stiff little voice from the doorway.

CHAPTER 9

Dinah's Secret

Dinah had not expected them to be nice to her. It had cost her quite a lot to push the door open. But at the sight of Harvey sobbing among the cushions, she was sure she had done the right thing.

'Please may I see the sums?'

'No you may not!' Lloyd snapped. 'You only want to gloat, don't you? You're just a mean, horrible –'

Harvey raised a tear-stained face from the cushions. 'Oh, let her,' he said wearily. 'What difference can it make? *I* don't think she's horrible enough to gloat, even if you do. There you are, Di. There are the beastly sums. On the floor.'

Dinah bent down and picked up the pieces of paper. Her cheeks had turned red and her heart was thudding uncomfortably. *Be quiet!* a voice in her head was saying. *Don't be too clever. Don't give yourself away.* She looked at Harvey and then at Lloyd's wretched, worried face. And then at the sums.

'Aren't they impossible?' Lloyd said.

Dinah took a deep breath. 'There's no way either of you could do them.'

'Ha, ha,' Lloyd sneered. 'And I suppose you could, clever clogs.'

'Yes,' Dinah said slowly. 'Yes, I can.'

Lloyd stared at her.

'It's all right, Harvey,' said Dinah. '*I can do your sums.*'

There was total silence. Harvey's mouth fell open and Lloyd went on staring.

'I can do them,' Dinah said again.

Harvey sat up, blinking at them. His hair flopped over his eyes and his cheeks were red.

'Honest?'

'Honest,' said Dinah reluctantly. 'Give me a pen and some paper and I'll do them now.'

She felt their eyes watching her as she sat down at the table and read the first sum.

'You need to use Probability Theory for that one,' she said briskly. Her eye travelled on down the page. 'And Spherical Geometry for that one. And this one – phew!' She whistled. 'You need Tensor Calculus for that. He *really* didn't mean you to do them, did he?'

'But *you* can do them?' Harvey said anxiously.

'I told you.' Her pen started to move across the paper and, behind her, she heard Lloyd gasp in disbelief. Taking no notice, she plunged into the sums, completely absorbed. One or two of the problems were so difficult that she had to think hard and she began to hum softly, enjoying herself. By the time she had finished, the two boys were staring at her with awed curiosity.

'How – how on earth did you do them?' Lloyd said awkwardly.

Dinah sat back in her chair. 'I'm clever.'

Lloyd's mouth twitched, as if he were going to jeer, and she laughed suddenly. 'No, I'm not boasting. I'm *really* clever. At sums and all sorts of things like that.'

'Nobody told us,' Lloyd said sulkily.

'Nobody knows.' Dinah pulled a face. 'Can't you imagine how other children would treat me? They'd be *beastly*. I found that out when I was about five. So – I decided to play stupid. I kept quiet and I just went on finding out about things by myself, at the library and so on. And no one's ever guessed. Nobody's known about me. Until now.'

Lloyd still looked dubious, but Harvey gave a sudden crow of delight. 'So you've done the rotten sums. Whoopee!' He jumped to his feet and did a little jig. 'I'm starving!'

'Should just think you are,' Lloyd said gruffly. 'After all that stupid fuss you made. Here – have this.' He pulled a Mars bar out of his pocket and tossed it over. Tearing off the paper, Harvey began to cram it into his mouth greedily, but Lloyd was still staring at Dinah.

'You didn't want anyone to know you were clever,' he said slowly, 'You've hidden it all these years. But you've told us now. Why?'

Dinah looked down at her fingers, feeling embarrassed. 'I couldn't let Harvey — well, I was sorry for him.'

'But we've been foul to you!'

She grinned wryly. '*You've* been foul to me. Harvey's been quite nice.'

Lloyd frowned. 'But it doesn't make any sense. You've just got Harvey out of trouble. But it was you that got him into it. It must have been you that told about him going into school early and spying on the Assembly. No one else knew.'

Dinah shook her head. 'It wasn't me that told. Anyway, Rose saw him going in for the registers. She was watching through the window. Perhaps someone saw him outside the Hall as well.'

'But you lied about the snowballs, and you keep saying how marvellous the school is, and telling about the films you see in Assembly. And it's all lies. You know it is. I can't understand you at all.'

Dinah put her face in her hands. 'It's worse than that,' she said slowly. Then she paused for a moment. Somehow, talking about it made it seem realer, more frightening. But if she did not talk about it now, she never would. She forced herself to go on. '*I* don't understand me. All those things you've described — they come out mechanically. Before I've decided what I'm going to say. And when I say how marvellous the school is — I know what I really think, but I can't say it.'

'But that's ridiculous.' Lloyd began to march up and down the room. 'Why should you say things you don't want to?'

Harvey had finished eating the Mars bar and was watching them both with quiet interest. All of a sudden, he said, 'Assembly.'

'What?' Lloyd stopped pacing and looked at him. 'What do you mean?'

Harvey wiped his chocolate-covered fingers on the arm of the chair. 'It must be something to do with Assembly. It's the only place Dinah goes where neither of us does. What happened in Assembly today, Di?'

'In Assembly this afternoon,' Dinah chanted, 'we saw a film about coal-mines and –' She clapped a hand over her mouth and, with a visible effort, stopped speaking.

'That's right,' Harvey said. 'You didn't. I felt so rotten this afternoon I hardly did any work. Just looked out of the window. And the lights never went out.'

Dinah looked distressed. 'Don't you see?' she said urgently. 'It's the same thing again. I've said that something happened. A long explanation that came reeling out before I could think about it. And you say it's not true. Just like you said about the snowball fight.'

'And we're right,' insisted Lloyd.

Slowly, Dinah nodded. 'I think you might be. But why should I say these things? And if we don't see films in Assembly – what happens?' Her eyes were big and worried.

'You must remember, Di,' Harvey said. 'If you were there, you must remember it somehow, with some part of your brain. Go on. Remember it, remember it.'

'Say that again,' Dinah muttered, in an odd voice.

Harvey was puzzled. 'I just said – go on, remember it, remember it.'

'Go *on*,' Dinah said. 'Don't stop. It's coming.'

'Remember it, remember it, remember it,' chanted Harvey.

Dinah's forehead creased, as if she were making a mammoth effort.

'Remember it, remember it, remember it.'

As if she were in a daze, she started to mumble and stutter. 'Hyp –, hyp –, hypno –'

Then her face flooded with joyful excitement. 'Hypnotism!' she yelled, banging her fist down on the table. 'That's it! Hypnotism.'

Lloyd looked at her doubtfully.

'That's it!' she said again, her eyes glowing. 'The first day, when I went into Assembly, I didn't look at the Headmaster's eyes when the others did. I closed mine. And I heard him hypnotize everyone else. But then he caught me. I just had time to think *remember it, remember it* – and then I was hypnotized and I forgot. Until Harvey brought it back. *The Headmaster hypnotizes everyone in Assembly.*' She stared round triumphantly at them.

'But why?' Harvey said dubiously. 'What's the point?'

Dinah shrugged. 'It's a good way to keep everyone in order. And you know how he likes order. While they're hypnotized, he tells them what to do when they wake up. And they can't help doing it. Like me saying those things. And I think –' she paused, considering '– I think he probably makes us learn things, parrot-fashion, while we're hypnotized. Then, when we're awake, we can remember them and write them down.'

'A quick way to produce a school full of geniuses,' Lloyd said sourly. But Dinah shook her head.

'We're not learning to *think*. We're just learning to repeat things. Like robots. It looks good, but it's no use at all.'

Harvey shuddered. 'It's horrible.'

'It's all right for you,' Dinah said. 'He doesn't do it to you. I wonder why not.'

'He can't,' Harvey said. 'We're invulnerable.'

He was only joking, but Dinah looked serious. 'I think you might be right. Some people can't be hypnotized. Has he ever tried it with you? Gazed into your eyes and told you you were tired?'

'Yes,' Lloyd said slowly. 'He did once. When I first came to the school. He took off his glasses and stared at me and said, "Lloyd, you are very tired. You are very, very sleepy."'

'And what happened?'

'Nothing much. I just said, "No, sir, I'm fine, thank you."'

'So did I,' put in Harvey. 'He did it to me, too. I just thought he was being silly.'

'Oh no,' Dinah said slowly, 'I don't think he's silly at all. He's cruel and terrifying, and he's got an obsession with tidiness, but he's not silly. He's very, very clever. He's got a whole school full of children who will do precisely what he wants. He must feel very powerful.'

Her voice was awed. 'Very powerful,' she said again. 'If I were him, I don't think I'd be satisfied with having one measly school in my power!'

'What do you mean?' Harvey said.

She looked round at them. 'Think of it. He's got a whole army of people – people like me – who'll do and say exactly what he wants. Why should he stop there? Sooner or later, he's going to want to do something with his army.'

There was a long, tense pause. Then Harvey said, 'L, don't you think – we should bring the others in on this?'

Lloyd looked carefully at Dinah. 'Think she can be trusted?'

'Of course,' Harvey said impatiently. 'Look what she's just done for me.' He flapped the paper with the sums on. 'We'll swear her to secrecy. Tomorrow. After school.'

CHAPTER 10

SPLAT

'We always go in separately,' Lloyd said in a mysterious voice. 'Just in case anyone's watching. You go first, H. I'll bring Dinah in a moment.'

Harvey nodded and slipped away down an alley between the houses opposite. Lloyd prodded Dinah. 'Go on. Keep staring in the shop window. As if you're interested.'

'In baths and basins?' Dinah said lightly. 'Who'd believe that? Go on, Lloyd. Tell me what's happening.'

'Wait and see.' Lloyd looked even more mysterious. 'You'll find out soon enough.'

He went on examining a purple soap dish with every

appearance of enthusiasm for a couple more minutes. Then he glanced at his watch and looked up and down the road. 'OK. I think it's all right now. Come on.'

He led the way, with elaborate casualness, down the alley. At the bottom was a gate into a garden. He pushed it open and they were facing a little wooden shed. He rapped on the door.

'The man who can keep order can rule the world,' said a voice from inside.

Beside him, Lloyd felt Dinah start with surprise, and he grinned. 'But the man who can bear disorder is truly free,' he answered.

The wooden door opened. 'Pass, friend.'

He slid through, motioning Dinah to follow him. She bent her head sideways, to avoid the garden tools hanging round the opening, and walked in, to find herself confronting four pairs of eyes. Ian, Mandy and Ingrid looked frankly hostile. Only Harvey gave her an encouraging smile.

'Have a box.' He pushed one towards her, and she sat down, like the others, squashed uncomfortably close in the confined space. The shed was dark and dusty, and the box creaked perilously underneath her.

Ian looked at her, raising one elegant, fair eyebrow. 'Well, well, Lloyd,' he murmured. 'Who have you brought with you, then? I hope you have a good excuse.'

'He'd better have,' little Ingrid said hotly. 'He's broken all the rules and put us all in danger.'

Mandy smiled gently. 'Suppose we hear what he's got

to say. Lloyd doesn't usually do things without a good reason.'

Lloyd nodded. 'I'm glad Mandy said that. I didn't really want to bring Dinah, but I think she's got some important information to give you.'

'But she's one of Them,' Ingrid said crossly. 'One of the Headmaster's goody-goodies. Why should we believe anything she says?'

'You will when you've heard it,' Harvey broke in. 'Oh, go on, Di. Tell them.'

'Wait a minute.' Dinah had sat quietly, listening to them arguing. Now she sat up straighter. 'You want to know that I won't get you into trouble. That's fair enough. But how do I know that you won't get me into trouble? What is all this, and why do you meet here, in secret?'

Ingrid bridled again, but Ian said, 'It's a fair enough question. Why don't you explain, Mr Chairman? Now she's seen this much, it can't do any more harm.'

'All right,' Lloyd said. 'If no one minds.' He turned to Dinah. 'This is the Society for the Protection of our Lives Against Them.'

'SPLAT for short,' Harvey put in.

'Us against the Headmaster and the teachers and all the goody-goodies,' Ingrid said with relish. She frowned. 'And we're Us and you're one of Them, so I can't think what you're doing here.'

'But what do you *do*?' Dinah said.

Ian grinned. 'Ah, the crucial question. Well, we all keep an eye out for the prefects, so we can warn each other, and we swap details of all the new rules the Headmaster invents, so that we don't get caught out.'

'And Mandy helps us with our sums and things,' Ingrid added.

Mandy blushed. 'It's not just that, though. Mostly it's to keep our spirits up. So we don't feel we're all alone in the horrible school, with no one to help us.'

'I see.' Dinah nodded. 'Well, I think you'll feel better when you've heard what I want to say. You see –'

'Wait a moment.' Ian held up his hand. 'I think you should take the oath first. Mr Chairman?'

'Yes, of course,' Lloyd said shortly, annoyed that he had not thought of it himself. 'Dinah Glass, do you swear to honour the secrecy of SPLAT, to protect its members and never willingly to reveal anything about any of Us to any of Them?'

'I do,' Dinah said solemnly.

'Right,' said Lloyd. 'Now tell them.'

'It's about Assembly,' Dinah began. 'You see . . .'

She leaned forwards eagerly and began to explain, answering their questions clearly and briefly. Lloyd watched her. He supposed she could be trusted, but somehow he had not expected the others to believe her so quickly. If he had had to put in a good word for her, to plead for her to be heard, he would have felt more friendly towards her. But the others seemed to be on her side straight away. Rather crossly, he studied them.

Ian was looking at her with cool approval and Mandy was grinning her shy, pleasant grin. Even Ingrid had been convinced. She was still raging, but now her rage was all directed at the Headmaster. She bounced up and down on her box and banged her fist into the palm of her hand.

'He's *evil*! *Wicked*! Do you mean all the others are victims really? It's him that makes them behave like that? Oh, it's fiendish, it's –'

'Calm – down – Ingrid.' Ian patted her annoyingly on the back. 'Think how pleased the Headmaster will be if you choke to death.'

She stopped abruptly and everyone laughed. Lloyd decided that it was time he took charge of the meeting again. After all, he was the Chairman. But before he could say anything, Harvey burst out, 'But you haven't heard the most important part yet – what Dinah thinks.'

'She has important thoughts, does she?' Ian said teasingly.

Mandy gave a reproachful look. 'Of course she does. You heard Harvey say how clever she was. Come on, Di. What is it?'

'Well, I'm worried about what's going to happen next.' Earnestly, Dinah began to explain her fears about the Headmaster's plans.

Lloyd chewed irritably at the end of his finger. He had meant to do this bit himself. Get them all organized, the way he usually did. But it was no use interrupting yet. He waited until Dinah had finished and then rapped smartly on the floor to call the meeting to order.

'Right now, you've all heard what Dinah has to say. There's no evidence for it, of course, but it makes sense. The question is – what are we going to do about it?'

Mandy looked thoughtful. 'We really need a way of finding out what actually happens in Assembly. Apart from the hypnotism, I mean. If the Headmaster's going to use the children for anything, that'll be where he tells them all about it.'

'Can't you stay awake somehow, Di?' Ingrid said.

Dinah sighed. 'I told you. I've tried that. But he can tell.' She looked at them, one by one. 'But he can't hypnotize any of you. Couldn't one of you sneak into the Hall and hide?'

Ian shook his head. 'Not a chance. We always have a prefect watching us. They treat us as if we were criminals. I don't suppose they'll even let us go to the toilet. Not now they know what Harvey did.'

'Anyway,' Harvey said quickly, 'there's nowhere to hide in the Hall. You know what it's like.'

Dinah nodded silently and there was a long pause. Lloyd was straining to think of a good idea. He was usually the one with the brainwaves. He had taught the others to mouth, so that they could talk in secret when no one was looking. And he was the one who had started the Register of Rules and persuaded the others to copy bits out of encyclopaedias so that they could keep up with the goody-goodies at school. But now his mind felt like a piece of soggy cottonwool.

'It's a pity we can't bug the Hall,' he said at last, in a flippant voice.

'Lloyd – that's it!' Dinah bounced on her seat, looking unusually excited for her. Her cheeks were very faintly pink. 'We can't bug the Hall very easily, but we can bug *me*! Has anyone got a little tape-recorder? A battery one?'

'Yes,' Ian and Mandy said together.

'Well then, it's easy. I'll put it in my blazer pocket and turn it on when I go into the Hall. It won't record very well in there, but it'll probably pick up enough to tell us . . .'

She launched into a long discussion with Ian about the best way to do it. Mandy put in a suggestion from time to time and Harvey and Ingrid were nodding away in agreement.

Lloyd watched them all, totally disgusted. He might have known how it would be. He had told Harvey that there would never be any peace and quiet again if a girl came to live with them, and he had been right, for all she looked so meek and docile. There had been nothing but trouble ever since she walked into the house.

And now she had walked into her first SPLAT meeting – where she had no business to be anyway – and taken it over. No one would guess *he* was the Chairman, or that bugging the Hall had been *his* idea. He sat hunched over on his box, sulking.

Suddenly, Ingrid prodded him. 'Hey, wake up, Lloyd. We're taking a decision.' She turned to Dinah. 'It's one of our rules. Everything we do has to be agreed by all of us. Otherwise we don't do it. There are so few of us that we can't afford to argue.'

Grumpily, Lloyd looked round at them. 'Right, let's take a vote. The proposal is that Dinah should take a tape-recorder into Assembly. Ian? Harvey? Mandy? Ingrid?' All four of them nodded.

'And Dinah,' Harvey said. 'You've forgotten her. She's a sworn-in member too.'

'Dinah?' Lloyd said reluctantly.

Dinah nodded slowly, watching Lloyd's face. 'What about you?' she murmured. 'You haven't said anything yet.'

'I'm not sure I do agree,' Lloyd said. 'It's a very dangerous plan, and we've always tried to keep out of danger. That's what this society's for, not for solving mysteries. What happens if something goes wrong?'

'I'm the only one who'll be in danger then,' Dinah said mildly. 'If I'm not afraid, why should you be? I won't tell on the rest of you. I swore. Remember?'

'But how do we know you'll keep your promise?'

'Oh *L*!' Harvey said impatiently.

Lloyd could see the others growing annoyed with him as well. He would have to give in. 'All right, all right,' he said with bad grace. 'We'll try it. Tomorrow. And we'll all meet at our house afterwards, to listen to the tape. But I bet we don't find out anything useful.' Ingrid glared at him, and he banged on the floor again before she could say anything. 'Meeting dissolved.'

He stamped home at high speed, trying to leave Dinah behind. But Harvey chose to walk with her and chat, instead of catching up, and that did not improve Lloyd's temper one little bit.

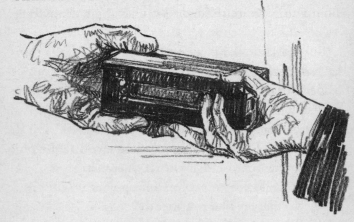

CHAPTER II

Dinah the Spy

*A*s Dinah swallowed her last mouthful of cheese flan, she felt more lonely than she had ever felt in her life before. All the other members of S P L A T were sitting together, on their usual isolated table in the dining hall, but they had decided that it would seem suspicious if she sat with them. So she was next to Lucy, on a table full of good, well-behaved pupils, all of them munching their way through the same-sized platefuls of cheese flan, watery cabbage and lumpy mashed potato. Chop, scrape, lift, chop, scrape, lift, went the knives and forks, in regular rhythm. No one complained about the terrible food. No one asked to leave any. No one spoke at all. Even Lucy was chewing stolidly.

Her stomach fluttering nervously, Dinah reached out for her dish of rice pudding. As she did so, she slipped her other hand into her pocket, feeling the shape of the little cassette recorder underneath the cover of her handkerchief.

'Dinah Glass!' said Rose's voice over her shoulder.

Dinah froze, rigid.

'Well?' Rose snapped.

'Well what?' muttered Dinah guiltily.

'Your knife and fork!'

Glancing at her empty plate, Dinah saw that she had left the knife and fork lying untidily askew. Trying not to look too relieved, she twitched them straight, so that they lay at the same neat angle as everyone else's. Then she ate her rice pudding quickly, feeling, with every mouthful, that she might choke with fright. The tape-recorder seemed to be making a gigantic bulge in her pocket, visible to anyone.

Ten minutes later, as if at a signal, everyone on her table stood up, ready to walk off to Assembly. Lloyd, Harvey and the others were still finishing their puddings. As Dinah passed their table, she glanced quickly sideways. Not one of them looked at her. But each of them had a hand on the table and, momentarily, they all crossed their fingers. Even Lloyd. Slightly comforted, Dinah marched out of the dining room and into the Hall and sat down beside Lucy, who gave her a cautious smile.

'Hallo,' Dinah whispered. 'How are things?'

Lucy smiled again and shrugged. Then, greatly daring,

she whispered back. 'How are you getting on?'

'Good question.' Dinah glanced round at Them, at the children and teachers, all of whom would give her away if they knew what she had in her pocket. She grinned wryly. 'I feel like Winston Smith.'

'Winston Smith?' whispered Lucy, puzzled.

'He was a man who was spied on all the time. In a book called *Nineteen Eighty-Four*.'

'Oh.' Lucy still looked bewildered. 'Funny name for a book.'

'It means –' Dinah started, but Lucy nudged her sharply.

'Ssh! Here he comes.'

The Headmaster was walking slowly up the middle of the Hall, his long gown swirling and his head erect. He looked neither to right nor to left, but as he passed all fidgeting stopped. Children sat up straighter in their chairs and faced the front. While he climbed the steps of the stage, the men teachers pulled their ties smooth and the women patted their hair.

'Good afternoon, school,' he said.

'Good afternoon, sir,' replied everyone, voices perfectly together.

He looked gravely down on the rows of heads in front of him and reached up to take off his glasses. Dinah felt a sudden spurt of revulsion at the thought of letting herself be hypnotized again. But there was nothing she could do. It had to happen if the plan was to succeed. Her finger, in her blazer pocket, twitched once, turning on the tape-recorder, and then the voice began.

'I'm pleased to learn that you have all been working very hard this morning. You have done well, but now you must be weary. Weary and sleepy . . .'

Crossing her fingers hard in her pockets, Dinah shut her eyes and felt the heavy, inexorable tide of sleep start to wash over her.

She was already unconscious when the Headmaster gave his first orders, so she never knew quite what happened next. She was not aware of the Headmaster's steady voice, nor of her own, repeating what they were all told to repeat. She could not even feel the shape of the tape-recorder, clutched tightly in her fingers, inside her pocket.

'Right!' said the Headmaster suddenly. 'Now move to the groups I divided you into yesterday and prepare to receive instructions.'

Their eyes open but glazed, two hundred children rose to their feet, completely silently except for the shuffling of chairs, and started to move along the rows like robots, rearranging themselves into six groups in different parts of the Hall.

Dinah's feet took her mechanically up on to the stage. As she walked across it, she passed the Headmaster, but although her eyes passed over his face she was not aware of the irritable way it twitched.

'Dinah Glass – stop.'

Obediently, she stood to attention.

'You look slovenly. Take your hand out of your pocket at once.'

Without any hesitation, she drew out her hand, still

tightly clutching the tape-recorder. The Headmaster had begun to turn away, but out of the corner of his eye he caught sight of it. He whirled back.

'Give me what you have in your hand.'

Her face blank and calm, Dinah held out the tape-recorder and he took it from her. For a moment or two, he turned it over thoughtfully in his hands.

'Well, well,' he said softly, 'so that's the way the wind blows, is it? I can see I shall have to deal with you at once, and not leave it until next week.' Briefly his fingers moved, pressing switches. Then he said in a louder voice, 'Mr Venables. Come here.'

Automatically, Mr Venables marched up on to the stage and, with an expression of careful calculation on his face, the Headmaster began to whisper in his ear.

When Dinah opened her eyes again, blinking, she had a second of complete, distracted panic. She was not quite sure where she was. Somehow, she had expected to be somewhere else . . . Then, gradually, the pieces of the room swam into place and she realized that she was sitting in her own classroom. It was totally empty, except for Mr Venables, who was at his desk, facing her.

'Good afternoon, Dinah,' he said briskly.

She blinked again. 'What – what am I doing here?'

'You are here because I have something to say to you. Come up to my desk.'

Still dazed, she stood up and walked towards him. It was only when she was standing beside the desk that she noticed what was lying on top of it. Three sheets of paper covered with sums worked in her own tiny figures. Very difficult sums. She was too controlled to catch her breath, but her face became completely wooden.

Mr Venables tapped the papers with one finger. 'You did these sums. Didn't you?'

'They were Harvey's sums, not mine,' Dinah said carefully. Mr Venables gave an impatient sigh.

'There was never any chance that Harvey could do them. They were set to see if you would do them to help him. If you *could* do them. And he will be punished for letting you help him unless –'

'But that's not fair!' Dinah broke in. 'He would have been punished if they weren't done and now he's going to be punished because they *are* done. He never had any chance.'

'Fairness is an illusion, designed to create disorder,' Mr Venables said calmly. 'Besides, I did not say that he would be punished. Only that he would be punished unless – unless you decide to help him by cooperating.'

Dinah stood stubborn and silent. Mr Venables looked at her.

'You are a clever girl, Dinah, however much you may have tried to hide it. You must see that you have no choice.'

'What do you want me to do?' she said stiffly.

Briskly, Mr Venables began to explain, and Dinah stared at him, completely amazed.

She walked home alone, in a dream, so wrapped up in what she was thinking that she did not see anything around her. When she pushed open the kitchen door,

Mrs Hunter smiled at her.

'The others are all in the playroom. They wondered what had happened to you.'

'The others?' Dinah said, still vague. Mrs Hunter looked at her.

'Are you all right, dear?'

'What? Oh yes.' Suddenly, Dinah remembered what was supposed to be happening. She slid her fingers into her pocket and felt the solid shape of the cassette recorder. 'I just walked home rather slowly, that's all.'

'Do you want something to eat?'

'No. No thanks. I'd better go and talk to them.'

As she reached the playroom door, a voice from inside said, 'The man who can keep order can rule the world.'

For one moment she could not drag the right reply out of her memory. Then it came. 'But the man who can endure disorder is truly free.'

Ingrid wrenched open the door excitedly. 'Hallo, Brains. What happened? Hey, you look terrible.'

Silently, Dinah walked in and put the tape-recorder down on the table. Mandy touched her hand gently.

'What's the matter? Did you get caught?'

'No. I mean, I don't know.'

'You don't know?' Lloyd spluttered. 'Christmas puddings! Don't be silly. You must know.'

'No she mustn't,' Ian said. 'She's been hypnotized. Remember? Let's listen to the tape.'

Dinah nodded. Best to get that over first. Then she could talk properly.

Ian reached for the switch, and they all sat watching

the tape run through for two or three minutes. Then he pressed another switch and ran it on a bit and they listened again.

There was no sound.

'You didn't switch it on!' Lloyd said accusingly. 'You forgot.'

'No I didn't. I remember doing it. I don't remember anything after that, but I did switch it on.'

'Perhaps it didn't pick up anything,' Mandy said soothingly. 'It was in her pocket, after all.'

Lloyd looked stubborn. '*I* think she mucked it up.'

'Oh, leave her alone!' Harvey thumped him. 'You're always getting at her, Lloyd. Look, you've upset her.'

'No,' Dinah murmured. 'No, it's not that. I don't know why the recording didn't work. But something else happened.'

Suddenly they were all looking at her curiously.

'Come on,' Ingrid urged. 'Don't spin it out. Tell us.'

Dinah took a deep breath.

'Why,' she said quietly, 'didn't anyone tell me that the school was going to be on the Eddy Hair Show next week? In the Great School Quiz?'

CHAPTER 12

'Got You Guessing?'

'Oh *that*?' Lloyd shrugged. 'Didn't you know about that? Why should we get excited about it? It only means more glory for the Headmaster. And none of *us* is going to be in the team. What's that got to do with anything?'

Typical of a girl, he thought. She was just trying to distract them, because she'd messed up the business with the tape-recorder.

But Dinah was staring at him as if he were an idiot. 'Can't you see how peculiar it is?' she said softly. 'Think what the Eddy Hair Show's like. Mess. Chaos. They fling things all over the place. Flour, soot, chickens – all sorts of things. Sometimes they even break windows.'

'I expect they pay for them afterwards,' Ian said.

'But look.' Dinah leaned forwards, anxious that they should see things her way. 'Think what the school's like. If you put your knife and fork down out of line, someone's on to you. If you throw snow at someone, the whole place goes mad. Why should the Headmaster have *invited* the Eddy Hair Show to come? Because he must have done.'

'You're right,' Mandy said slowly. 'I never thought of it like that before. It is odd.'

Lloyd banged the table. 'What does it matter if it's odd? It's got nothing to do with what we're talking about.'

'I'm not so sure,' Dinah said softly. 'You see – the Headmaster knows it was me that did those sums for Harvey.' Harvey gasped and she smiled at him reassuringly. 'No, it's all right. They were a trap. I was meant to do them. But so that you don't get into trouble for it – I've got to be in the Quiz team for the Eddy Hair Show.'

'So?' Lloyd said disagreeably. 'That just goes to prove what I've said all along. You're one of Them, not one of Us.'

'Oh, do be quiet!' For once, Ian was roused out of his usual lethargy, positively snarling at Lloyd. 'Can't you see Dinah's got more to say? And if she thinks it's important it must be worth listening to.'

Lloyd subsided, sulking, and Dinah went on, choosing her words carefully.

'It was Mr Venables who told me about being in the team. And the really odd thing was that he kept saying, "You must see to it that the team wins. The Headmaster says that the team *must* win. Otherwise, there'll be trouble for Harvey Hunter."'

'You can do it, can't you?' Harvey said, in a worried voice. 'You are clever enough, Di?'

'Oh, I expect so,' Dinah said vaguely. 'But that's not the point. The point is – why is the Headmaster so desperate for us to win? Why should it be important to him?'

Lloyd snorted. 'More honour and glory for his precious school.'

Dinah shook her head, frowning. 'No, I don't think that's it. It doesn't seem to fit, somehow. There's something else. Something at the back of my mind that makes it all make sense. But I can't catch hold of it.'

'Look,' Ian said suddenly. 'It's Friday today, isn't it? Well, the Eddy Hair Show's on at six o'clock. We'll watch it and see if that helps.'

'Oh, good-oh!' Ingrid chirped. 'I love it. Especially the Great School Quiz. The questions are so hard, I can never do any of them.'

'That's because we're all taught parrot-fashion,' said Dinah. 'The questions in the Quiz are puzzles, and no one in our school's encouraged to think. It's quite the wrong quiz for our sort of school. So why did the Headmaster get us into it?'

'It's just the fame he wants,' Lloyd said. 'I told you.

You know what they say about the Eddy Hair Show. Everyone in the country switches on at six o'clock on a Friday to watch it.'

'But –' began Dinah. Lloyd flung his hands up in despair, ready to argue with her.

'Let's forget it for now,' Mandy said hastily. 'Who's for a game of I-Spy?'

The television set flickered briefly and then the picture swelled into colour. Six girls, apparently with no heads, danced across the screen, chased by a large gorilla.

'Yes, folks,' said a cheerful voice from nowhere, 'it's what you've all been waiting for. Your weekly dose of craziness in a sane, sad world. The Great, the Magnificent, the *only* – EDDY HAIR SHOW!'

The gorilla jumped into a dustbin. Then it reached up and pulled its head off, revealing Eddy Hair's purple-painted face.

'It's all rubbish,' he said severely. 'Only idiots watch this show. Tests prove that ninety-nine point nine per cent of our viewers have no heads.'

Bounding from the dustbin, he waggled his purple hair at the audience. 'And just you wait till you see what a vintage load of rubbish is on the show today. If you had any sense, you'd switch off now. Got you guessing? *That's* how I like it!'

At manic speed, the show swung into its usual succession of gags, sketches and disasters. Some of it was pre-recorded, like the piece where Eddy Hair swung from a helicopter, dropping balloons shaped like fat ladies over a Beauty Contest. But most of it was live, and one or two of the disasters were obviously completely unexpected. Whatever happened, Eddy Hair laughed his raucous laugh and all over the country people fell about, clutching their sides helplessly.

Only in the Hunters' sitting room was there total, grim silence. All the members of S P L A T were watching the show like detectives, trying to see why the Headmaster was interested in it. And the more they watched, the more baffled they became.

At last, there was a fanfare of trumpets, accompanied by wild grunts from a pig.

'At last!' bellowed Eddy Hair. 'Now you'll see that the people round here are not only mad but stupid. It's – the Great School Quiz.'

Immediately, the cameras panned round the school hall where the show was taking place. Two teams, each of three children, were sitting facing each other and beside each, on a throne, sat a cheerful-looking Head Teacher. Eddy Hair walked across the stage with his knees knocking dramatically.

'Can't stand teachers!' he whispered at the camera. 'They terrify me.'

Then, with a grin, he was squatting on top of a barrel, reaching for the first question.

'Right. It's a question for the Manor Junior School. You have thirty seconds to think, and anyone can answer – *if* you're not all too thick to work it out. Here goes. "I want to buy roller skates for my chickens. Twelve per cent of them have only one leg, and half the rest refuse to wear roller skates. So how many skates do I need to buy?"'

'That's impossible,' Mandy said. 'He hasn't said how many chickens there are.'

'It's the same number of skates as the number of chickens,' Dinah said calmly. 'It works out to one leg each.'

Almost thirty seconds later, a brainy-looking boy with glasses faltered, 'The same as the number of chickens?'

Eddy Hair beamed at him. 'Watch you don't burn your mind out, genius. Thinking's bad for your football, remember. Now, the next question . . .'

As the Quiz went on, the questions grew harder and harder, but Dinah answered them all, hardly pausing to think. And the more she answered, the crosser Lloyd grew.

'Oh, shut up!' he yelled, as the last question was asked. 'We know you've got brains the size of the Eiffel Tower. No need to rub it in. I vote we turn off this stupid programme.'

'Not yet,' wailed Ingrid. 'It's just getting to my favourite bit. With the Head Teachers. Let's watch that.'

On the screen, Eddy Hair was waggling a finger at the Headmaster of Shillingstone Street School.

'Your lot,' he said cheerfully, 'are the Dimmest School of the Week. Prepare to receive your reward.'

In a flash, a giant panda appeared behind the Headmaster's chair and tipped a bucketful of flour over his head. As he emerged from the white cloud, brushing it from his beard, his pupils cheered wildly.

'I can just see our Headmaster liking that,' Ian said with relish. 'Perhaps the whole thing will be fun.'

'No,' murmured Mandy. 'We're going to win. Remember?'

'That's even better,' chuckled Ingrid. 'Do listen. What's the other Headmaster going to say?'

For Eddy Hair was now pointing at the Headmaster of the winning school.

'You seem to have a crowd of geniuses,' he said sourly. 'Suppose you tell us how you do it.'

This Headmaster was a large, cheerful man with a red face. The camera panned in on him, so that his face filled the whole screen.

'Doughnuts,' he said, perfectly gravely. 'We fill them full of doughnuts every morning before school. Good for the brain. You should try some, Eddy. And if anyone refuses to eat the doughnuts, we . . .'

He went on for a full minute, with the camera to himself, explaining the magical qualities of doughnuts, before the panda reappeared and jammed three doughnuts into his open mouth.

Lloyd reached forward and switched off the set. 'You see?' he said contemptuously. 'There's nothing for us to go on. It's just a red herring that Dinah's dreamed up.'

'Wait.' Dinah had gone white, and she was still staring at the empty screen, with her mouth open. Then, as if she were being strangled, she said, 'It's always like that, isn't it? The Headmaster of the winning team gets a whole minute to talk. To say whatever rubbish comes into his head. With most of the people in the country watching.'

Ian nodded.

'Well.' Dinah gulped. 'Think what our Headmaster could do with that.'

Mandy gasped.

'Would a minute be enough?' Harvey said.

'Probably.' Dinah considered. 'I don't think it took him nearly as long as a minute to hypnotize me the first time.'

'But that's *devilish*!' spluttered Ingrid. 'He'd have the whole country in his power. Do you think that's really what he's planning?'

'I don't see how he could resist it,' Dinah said miserably. 'Do you, Lloyd?'

Lloyd would dearly have liked to say she was wrong. Just to show her up. But the more he thought about it, the more certain it seemed. 'I think you've got it,' he said grudgingly.

'But *why*?' Dinah chewed her bottom lip.

Lloyd jumped to his feet. 'That's obvious! Don't be so dumb, Dinah. He'll be able to make his fortune. All he has to do is to tell everyone to send him a hundred pounds, or go out and rob a bank, or something. He'll be the richest man in the world.'

'Of course!' said Ian and Harvey together.

But Dinah looked doubtful. 'I'm not sure. It doesn't seem quite –'

'Oh, you!' Lloyd said bitterly. 'You want to have all the inspirations. Just because I thought of this one –'

Mandy interrupted him, ready to make peace as always. 'I can't see that it matters why he's doing it. The important thing is — what are we going to do about it?'

'Couldn't Dinah just lose the Quiz?' Ingrid said helpfully.

'No!' Harvey went white. And Dinah shook her head as well.

'That's too dangerous. He planned all this before I came, so he must have some scheme even if the team loses. No, the only safe thing is to stop the Eddy Hair Show coming to the school at all.'

'Right.' Lloyd decided that they had all listened to her for long enough. His head was suddenly bursting with ideas, and he was determined to take charge. 'I'm the Chairman, and I'm going to make the plans.' Everyone looked round at him and he grew more confident. This was better. Like before Dinah came. Everyone waiting for him to tell them what to do. 'We'll keep quiet for a week. So that no one suspects anything. Then, on the day of the show, this is what will happen . . .'

CHAPTER 13

SPLAT Goes into Action

*W*hen Lloyd, Harvey and Dinah arrived at school the next Friday morning, there was something slightly different about the atmosphere in the playground. A feeling of suppressed excitement. No one pranced about, or did imitations of Eddy Hair, or boasted about being in the Quiz team. The children were standing in their usual circles, chanting away. But the chant was a bit faster and, from time to time, people looked at each other, breathlessly. It was plain what they were thinking. At six o'clock that evening they would be sitting in the Hall and they would be on television.

The members of SPLAT kept well away from each

other. There was no need to speak. They knew what they had to do. For a whole week, they had been going over it at their meetings until the arrangements were perfect. This morning there were only five of them in the playground. Ian had hidden on the way to school, ready to carry out the first part of Lloyd's plan, and Mandy carried a note, forged by Dinah, which said that Ian would not be at school that day because he had a cold.

As the prefects gathered on the steps and the children started to move into line, Lloyd glanced round quickly to check that Mandy and Ingrid were there. As he glanced at them, they crossed their fingers quickly and moved off. Lloyd drew a deep breath. Nothing must go wrong. He only hoped that he had thought of everything.

The big outside-broadcast lorries trundled through the town, carrying the equipment needed to set up that evening's Eddy Hair Show. Inside, the drivers and technicians were laughing and chatting to each other. This was the easy part of their job. Once the show started, they were tense, not knowing what was going to happen from one moment to the next. Whatever Eddy Hair sprang on them, they had to cope with, somehow. But if they got the cameras and lights and microphones set up in good time, they could cope with anything.

At the traffic lights in the middle of the town, the first driver paused and pulled out a map. 'Right,' he said. 'We turn left here, and –'

He stopped suddenly. A tall, fair-haired boy in immaculate school uniform was jumping up and down beside his cab, trying to attract his attention. He wound the window down and leaned out. 'Yes, sonny?'

Ian put on his most virtuous and reliable expression. 'Are you the television people? Coming to do the Eddy Hair Show at our school?'

'Yes, that's right. You looking for us?'

Ian nodded. 'The Headmaster sent me. He asked if you would take the lorries round the back way. You go left here, right up the little lane, over the bridge and – Here, would you like me to come along and show you? I've got to go back to school anyway.'

'Sure. Hop up.' The driver grinned at him. 'Nice to come to a school where we get looked after so well.'

Ian climbed up into the cab and began to direct. Behind, he heard the other lorries start up and his mouth went dry. If only it worked. If only they did not suspect anything.

'Left here,' he said, his voice completely calm. 'Then right.'

'You're sure you've got it straight, sonny?' As the man beside him swung the wheel, he glanced sideways, doubtfully. 'I don't see any sign of a school.'

'That's all right,' Ian said airily. 'You can't see it from here. Go through those gates, and I'll hop out and tell the Headmaster you've come. Then you can bring the lorries up to the door one by one.'

Still frowning, the driver turned the wheel again. Slowly the lorry crunched through a pair of tall gates into the disused quarry. In front of them, tall cliffs of chalk stretched up on every side, cutting off any view.

Ian threw the door open and slipped down, out of the cab.

'Wait here. Won't be a moment.'

As he ran back to the entrance, the other two lorries were rolling through the gates. He waved cheerfully at the drivers and waited until they were clear, then began to shove at the heavy gates. For one panicky moment, he thought they were not going to move, but they swung together suddenly, with a clang, and he pulled out of his pocket the two big padlocks that Lloyd had given him. Quickly, he clipped them shut.

'Hey!' said a voice from inside the quarry. 'What're you doing?'

Not waiting to hear any more, Ian ran off down the road. Mission One was safely completed. Now came the tricky bit. He found the bush where he had hidden a bottle of cooking oil, pulled it out and set off towards the school. Somehow, he had to sneak in and out again, without being seen.

Mandy and Ingrid were not feeling so cheerful. Their part of the plan was next, but they had to wait until the end of the afternoon to start it, and they were not at all sure that it would work. They sat in their separate classrooms, biting their nails, and when they met at lunchtime, Mandy whispered, 'I'm scared. Suppose it all goes wrong?'

Ingrid glanced round to see if anyone was watching, then thumped her crossly. 'It had better not go wrong. You know what Lloyd said. We must get all possible enemies out of the way. Now shut up about it. I'll see you outside the staffroom at four o'clock.'

Mandy fretted her way through the afternoon, but at four o'clock she was standing bravely in the corridor outside the staffroom when Ingrid appeared.

'There's a terrible racket going on in the Headmaster's office,' Ingrid whispered. 'He's on the phone to the television headquarters, wanting to know why the cameras and things haven't arrived. I could hear him right through the door.'

Mandy grinned. 'At least Ian's first bit went OK. Let's hope the second bit did too, or we might be in trouble. All the teachers are in the staffroom. I've been watching them go in. Give me a couple of minutes to get down to the swimming pool and then knock on the door.'

She ran off, and a minute or two later, Ingrid rapped sharply on the staffroom door, panting as if she had been hurrying. When Mr Venables opened it, she began to speak quickly.

'Please, sir, I've got a message from the Headmaster. Eddy Hair wants to talk to all the teachers in the swimming pool building.'

'The swimming pool?' Mr Venables raised his eyebrows.

'It's a stunt he's got planned.' Ingrid gave her most innocent, frightened smile. 'He wants you all to join in, and the Headmaster's sounding rather cross and –'

Her lip trembled, from genuine nervousness, and that appeared to convince Mr Venables. He called over his shoulder, 'Come on, everyone. We've got to go down to the swimming pool. Some mad stunt of Eddy Hair's.'

Groaning wearily, the teachers began to emerge from the staffroom. They trooped out of the building and across the playground, towards the single-storey block where the swimming pool was housed. When they were halfway there, Ingrid said anxiously, 'Oh, do please hurry. *Run*. The Headmaster was *so* impatient!'

The group of teachers broke into a trot, making for the open door of the swimming pool. As the first few of them hurried through the door, their feet slipped on the oil which Ian had spread carefully all over the tiles. Slithering towards the water, they began to yell, but this only brought the other teachers running faster. As the last of them slipped through the door, the splashes began. One after another, they fell into the swimming pool, skidding uncontrollably over the edge.

Immediately, Mandy appeared from her hiding place round one corner, waving the swimming pool key. As Ingrid pushed the doors shut, she slid it into the lock. The shouting, splashing teachers had still not realized that they were not involved in one of Eddy Hair's crazy pranks. It would be some time before they discovered that they were prisoners. Ingrid winked at Mandy. 'That should keep them busy. Let's get out of here.'

At the same moment, Lloyd and Dinah were crouching round the corner from the prefects' room, quarrelling in whispers.

'They're not all there,' Dinah was saying. 'Rose and

Jeff are still around the school somewhere. If we don't get them, it could be very dangerous.'

'Don't be so bossy.' Lloyd frowned. 'All the other four are there, but they might come out once they've eaten their sandwiches. And if we don't lock them in and get down to the Hall, someone's going to notice that we're not eating ours. We'll just have to do without Rose and Jeff.'

'But they're the worst.'

'Oh, shut up!' Lloyd knew she was right really, but it did not make him better tempered. 'You're always interfering.'

Dinah shut her mouth tight. No use saying she had only been trying to help. She knew what Lloyd was like now. He wanted to be in charge all the time. Well, let him. She did not really think trapping the prefects would make any difference anyway.

'Go on, then,' she said quietly. 'Let's get it over with.'

Like a shadow, Lloyd stepped forwards and locked the door of the prefects' room. Then he put his ear to it.

'Hey,' he mouthed, 'they're saying something.'

Dinah came up beside him. Through the wood of the door, she heard Simon's voice reciting, as if he had learnt it by heart, 'And I take charge of transport. With twenty children to help me. According to Master Plan, Section C.'

Lloyd frowned. 'What are they on about?' he said noiselessly.

Dinah put a finger to her lips and leaned closer, hearing Sarah's voice now.

'I'm in charge of work camps. Master Plan, Section F. With fifty children to help. All people to be split up according to age. Museums and public buildings to be used for housing them and –'

'Oh, come on.' Lloyd pulled Dinah's sleeve. 'I don't know what they're up to, but it doesn't sound as though it's got anything to do with today. Let's go and eat our sandwiches. Then we can sneak off again and see how Harvey's doing.'

Dinah dragged her ear away from the door, feeling frustrated. She was sure she was missing something very important, but Lloyd was right. They could not risk being seen with their ears to the door.

'OK,' she said. 'They sound as though they'll go on talking for hours. And I don't suppose it'll matter about Rose and Jeff.'

'Of course it won't matter,' Lloyd said angrily. But he was not very happy as they crept off down the corridor. It was the first thing that had gone wrong.

Back in the middle of the town again, Ian was beginning to grow restless. Perhaps he had missed Eddy Hair. He might have been looking for the wrong sort of person. Perhaps the purple curls were just a wig and the crazy clothes were only for wearing on television. In that case, Eddy Hair could have slipped past a hundred times without being noticed. What an idiot he was not to have thought of that before! He frowned, and marched up and down by the traffic lights, stamping his feet to keep them warm.

Then he saw it. A little, low sports car, zooming along the main road towards him. There was no mistaking it. Even if the number plate had not been EH 1. Even if the car had not been painted in stripes of red, yellow and mustard colour. For there, at the wheel, was Eddy Hair himself, his huge bunch of purple curls almost filling the windscreen and a cheerful grin on his loony face.

Bounding with relief, Ian started to leap up and down beside the red traffic light, ready with his next set of false directions.

And for a moment it looked as though it was going to work. The sports car squealed to a stop and Eddy Hair leaned over and wound down the window.

'Please –' Ian started.

But Eddy Hair was obviously used to being stopped by waving children. He did not even give Ian a chance to finish his sentence. Instead, beaming all over his face, he shouted, 'Want an autograph, do you? Bless you, boy, you don't suppose I can *write*, do you?'

With a great screech of laughter, he banged the car into gear, roared the engine and was away as the lights changed, leaving only a cloud of exhaust fumes.

'Blast it,' Ian said softly. 'Blast, blast, blast!'

Then he began to run as fast as he could towards the school. He had to warn the others that the plan was not working perfectly. Luckily, he knew where he would find them all.

In the school boiler room, Harvey was shaking with fright, reading over and over again the instructions that

Dinah had given him. 'It's quite safe if you do it in the right order,' she had said firmly. 'But if you don't, you might kill yourself.'

He looked at his watch. Why didn't the others come? It was after half past four. He could not leave it any longer. Oh well, he would have to do without their help. Pulling a torch out of his pocket, he looked nervously up at the big red handle on the wall which said MAINS SUPPLY.

'Here goes,' he murmured.

Gripping the handle tightly with his right hand, he pulled it hard down.

Instantly, the cellar was pitch black. Harvey switched on the torch and wrenched open the door of the fuse box. With his left hand he began to tug out the fuses, cramming them into his pockets.

There was a quick clatter of feet outside the door. Glancing nervously over his shoulder, he saw Mandy and Ingrid run in.

'Smashing!' Ingrid said enthusiastically. She leaped for the fuse box. 'We'll give you a hand.'

As her fingers reached for a fuse, Lloyd and Dinah came creeping in.

'OK, H?' Lloyd muttered. 'Everything else is going according to plan. Well – nearly. Ian's on his way. I saw him racing through the gate while we were on our way up here. Now let's get a move on with those fuses. Once we've chucked them away, they won't be able to do anything, even if they do get the lights and cameras here.'

They had just cleared the fuse box when Ian arrived.

He pulled a face, gasping for breath. 'I couldn't stop Eddy Hair,' he panted. 'He really is as crazy as he seems on TV. But I've got the lorries locked up in the quarry OK, and – hey, Harvey!'

Harvey's hand, holding the torch, had begun to shake wildly, flashing light distractingly into everyone's eyes.

'Knock it off, Harvey!' Lloyd snapped. 'We've got to get out of here.'

'B – b – but –' stuttered Harvey, 'oh – look!'

He gestured despairingly towards the door, and the others spun round.

There, outlined in the doorway, was a tall figure in a gown. On either side of him stood Rose and Jeff, smirking.

'Well, well,' said the Headmaster. 'You've all been *very* busy today, haven't you?'

CHAPTER 14

The Headmaster in Control

For a whole minute there was complete, horrified silence in the crowded boiler room. Then the Headmaster said, very quietly, 'Put the fuses back.'

'We won't!' Ingrid shouted. 'You're evil and wicked and we won't do anything to help you.'

The Headmaster smiled. 'I think you will.' He raised his voice slightly. 'Children – come along to the door.'

There was a tramping of feet in the corridor outside and suddenly the space behind the Headmaster was full of faces with blank, glazed eyes. Thirty or forty hypnotized children.

'We'd better do it,' Ian groaned. 'Otherwise they'll just make us. Come on, everyone.'

Despairingly, they began to push the fuses back into the box. Then Harvey switched on the mains supply again and they were all blinking in the sudden glare of light.

'That's better,' said the Headmaster, in a satisfied voice. 'Now we had better repair the rest of the damage you have done. Rose, where are all the teachers?'

'I saw Mandy and Ingrid lock them into the swimming pool.'

'And the prefects, Jeff?'

'Locked in their room,' Jeff said.

The Headmaster nodded and glanced back at the miserable members of S P L A T. 'I have had you watched, you see. I am not entirely stupid. The only thing I did not know was what had happened to the camera crew. But from what I heard as we arrived, I would guess that they are shut up in the old quarry. If you are sensible, you will hand over all the keys to me. Now.'

Sullenly, Lloyd, Ian and Mandy tossed the keys on to the floor. At a signal from the Headmaster, Rose and Jeff scooped them off and ran away down the corridor. The Headmaster did not speak again until the sound of their feet had died away. Then he stepped further into the room and looked at Dinah.

'I think,' he said, 'that we had better discuss what is going to happen next.'

'I know what you want,' Dinah said stiffly. 'You want me to win the Great School Quiz for you. So that you can have a chance to hypnotize everyone in the country. Well, I won't do it. If it's the only way to stop you, I'll make sure I get all the questions wrong.'

The Headmaster raised his eyebrows. 'You have worked things out very cleverly. I can see that I have not over-estimated your intelligence. But you have under-estimated my determination. You cannot refuse to do what I want.'

'Can't I?' Dinah stepped forward belligerently, but the Headmaster did not look in the least worried. Turning to the children massed in the doorway, he snapped at them in a brisk voice.

'Listen to my orders. In front of you are six straw dolls. They are no longer needed. You will advance on them and,' he drew a deep breath, 'you will tear them to pieces.'

Simultaneously, all the children swivelled their eyes to look into the boiler room. They showed no signs of recognition. It was plain that they were seeing precisely what they had been told to see. As they started to advance. Dinah watched Lucy, who was in the middle of the front row. Her face was as calm and cheerful as if she had been going out to pick daisies.

Knowing it would be no use, Dinah began to yell at her as the children marched into the boiler room.

'Lucy! It's me, Dinah! And there's Lloyd and Harvey and the others. You can't hurt us!'

'She won't hear you,' the Headmaster said icily. 'She is programmed to listen only to me and the prefects.'

Dinah and the others cowered against the wall behind

them as the children came steadily tramping towards them.

'Think, Dinah, think!' Lloyd yelled. 'There must be some way out of this. Otherwise they'll kill us.'

The foremost children had reached them now. Slowly they raised their arms, hands outstretched like claws.

'Oh, help!' Harvey yelled. 'Someone, help!'

The claw-like hands grabbed. Dinah found her blazer gripped firmly by Lucy and she heard Mandy's blouse rip. From beside her, Ingrid wailed, 'Oh, I'm frightened.'

More and more hands were pulling at them. Glancing across the room, Dinah saw the Headmaster smiling calmly, with no sign of wavering. Coldly, she realized that he would not relent. If he had to kill them, he would kill them. As someone started to tug at her hair, she shouted, 'All right, I'll do it! Whatever you say! Just stop them!'

At once, with a triumphant smile, the Headmaster said softly, 'Stop, children.'

Slowly, the arms dropped. Mandy gave a quick gasp of relief and Harvey drew a sobbing breath.

'You will be in the Quiz?' the Headmaster murmured.

Dinah nodded, hanging her head.

'And you will win?'

'If that's what I have to do.'

'Very well.' The Headmaster's mouth twisted in an unpleasant expression. 'But do not suppose that I shall be so foolish as to trust you. Your friends will be in the Hall, surrounded by these children. If you break your promise, all I have to do is to say, "Destroy the dolls!" and they will be dead. Is that clear?'

Dumb with despair, Dinah nodded again. Beside her, she heard Lloyd's familiar snort, comforting in its ordinariness.

'We may not be able to stop you,' Lloyd said scornfully, 'but we still think you're wicked. Wicked and pathetic. Fancy being prepared to *kill* us. Just for money.'

For the first time, the Headmaster looked startled. 'What do you mean?'

'That's what you're after, isn't it?' Lloyd said stoutly. 'You want to hypnotize everyone so that you can get their money and be the richest man in the world. Well, I think it's pathetic.'

To their amazement, the Headmaster suddenly flung back his head and laughed, soundlessly and horribly. When he stopped, he shook his head at them sadly.

'Money? Oh yes, I should be really pathetic if that was all I wanted. No wonder you have been my enemies. No wonder you think I am wicked.'

'Well you are, aren't you?' Ingrid said stoutly. He shook his head at her again.

'No, I am not wicked. My plans are for the good of everyone.' His voice rose, almost hysterically. 'My plans are glorious and splendid!'

'But you aren't going to tell us what they are?' said Dinah.

'You will see soon. Very soon now.' He looked round at them all. 'And when you do, you will understand how wrong you have been. Until then, I must remember that it is the fate of great men always to be misunderstood. Now – let us go to the Hall.'

They began to walk along the corridor, the Headmaster gripping Dinah's shoulder and the others marching in the middle of the crowd of hypnotized children. As she walked, Dinah was thinking busily. What was it that the Headmaster wanted? He, at least, must believe that it *was* good. But – *what was it*?

In the Hall, everything was in chaos. The television men had just arrived and they were leaping about at high speed, hanging lights, positioning microphones and connecting wires. In the centre of it all, a wiry figure with a crop of purple curls was dancing wildly from place to place.

'Come on, lads!' Eddy Hair was shouting. 'You can just do it. If you work hard.'

The Headmaster walked straight up the middle of the Hall, with all the children following. Dinah saw his face twitch with distaste as he stared round at the crazy scene. Then he forced a jovial smile and tapped Eddy Hair on the arm.

'Aaaagh!' With a scream, Eddy Hair fell to the ground as if he had been shot. 'You got me!' He lay on the floor, looking up at the Headmaster.

'I beg your pardon,' the Headmaster said gravely. 'I didn't mean to startle you.'

'Good for the soul, being startled,' chuckled Eddy Hair. 'Nothing like the unexpected for keeping people on their – T O E S!' As he said the last word, he bounded to his feet. 'What can I do for you, O Master?'

'Do you want me to bring the school into the Hall yet?'

'Why not, why not?' Eddy Hair flapped a hand. 'Good for the lads here to have an audience. And I don't suppose they'll be finished until thirty seconds before the show starts. No time to set the audience up then. Yes, get the kids in now. And have your Quiz team ready at the side of the stage. But make sure they're all quiet. We don't want a racket.'

'Oh yes,' the Headmaster said, with an amused smile, 'I think I can assure you that all my pupils will be perfectly quiet.'

Dinah stood at the side of the stage, out of range of the cameras, with the rest of the children taking part in the Quiz. It had not occurred to her to wonder before who would be picked to make up the rest of the team. Now she discovered that it was to be Rose and Lucy. Rose was her usual unpleasant self, but Lucy, woken out of her hypnotized trance, was bubbling with excitement, hardly able to keep silent. She grinned merrily at Dinah. It was all that Dinah could do to grin back.

You nearly killed me an hour ago, she thought. But, looking at Lucy now, she found it almost impossible to believe. And if she could barely believe it, who else would?

The Manor Road Quiz team had just arrived and Lucy smiled at the boy with glasses. 'You're Alec Bates, aren't you?' she whispered. 'I saw you on television last week. You were very good.'

The boy grinned back at her, cockily. 'I've been prac-
tising since then. I'm even better now. You'll never beat
us.'

One of the sound engineers frowned at them and
wagged a finger. 'Ssh,' he said loudly. 'The show's just
about to start.'

As the first notes of the opening music filled the Hall,
Dinah craned her neck to see what was going on. In the
front row of chairs were the other members of SPLAT,
surrounded by wooden-faced children, all ready to attack
them if the instruction was given. She shuddered and
looked sideways at the Headmaster, who was next to
her.

He was staring across at the stage. Out there,
Eddy Hair had begun a fight with a giant plateful of
spaghetti. And the spaghetti was fighting him back,
huge white strands slapping slimily round his neck
and spoonfuls of sauce splattering messily all over the
stage. The Headmaster's face was white. His fingers
twitched and he looked as though he were going to
be sick.

He can't stand it, thought Dinah suddenly. *Mess actually
makes him ill.* Somehow, that thought was rather comforting. At least he had weaknesses. The knowledge made
her feel bold and, in a very soft voice, she asked the
question that had been bothering her for days. 'If you
hadn't got me in the school, how would you have
arranged to win the Quiz?'

The Headmaster dragged his eyes away from the stage,
and glanced at the other team. 'I should have hypnotized

them and made them lose,' he murmured. 'But I shan't have to do that now. Shall I?'

'No. No, of course not,' Dinah said quickly, afraid. But she was not too afraid to risk another question. 'And what *will* you do after – after you've had your minute on television?'

But he just smiled at her and turned back to the stage, with a shudder. Eddy Hair had started to fling pepper at the spaghetti. He had three or four huge scarlet pepperpots with black stripes and he was shaking them frantically, spraying showers of pepper everywhere. And the spaghetti was sneezing. Its pale strands whirled everywhere like the arms of an octopus.

Dinah was left to wonder, desperately, what was going to happen. She was so deep in her own thoughts that she jerked with shock when the sound engineer prodded her.

'Quick!' he said. 'On to the stage.'

'What?'

'Didn't you hear? The Quiz is about to start.'

CHAPTER 15

The Great School Quiz

*L*loyd, slumped in his chair at the front of the Hall, watched as the two teams filed out. The stage was a disgusting mess. Bits of spaghetti, broken eggs and torn paper lay all over the floor. On Dinah's chair lay one of the huge scarlet pepperpots which Eddy Hair had used in his fight with the spaghetti. Lloyd saw Dinah pick it up and put it on the table in front of her while the Headmaster, with an expression of revulsion, kicked away a squashed banana from near his foot.

'Ghastly, isn't it?' Eddy Hair said cheerfully. 'The

125

country must be in a mess when a show like this is so popular.'

He began to explain the rules of the Quiz. 'Ten questions for each team, with thirty seconds to answer. *If* you can.'

Dinah sat in her chair, with her hands clasped on the table in front of her. On her face was an expression of complete, total wretchedness. *It's worse for her than it is for us*, Lloyd thought suddenly. *We've only got to wait, but she's got to help him win.* He felt a sudden burst of pity for her and was surprised at himself. Was he getting soft?

'Right.' Eddy Hair reached for the question paper. 'Manor Road School first, and it's a real brain-buster. "King Zonk of Zoldovia has a hundred children. Ninety per cent of them have curly noses, eighty-five per cent of them are bald, eighty per cent of them have one leg and seventy-five per cent of them lisp. How many bald, one-legged, lisping children with curly noses must he have?"'

Wow! thought Lloyd. But Alec Bates was already smiling confidently and scribbling on the paper in front of him. A moment later, he had answered.

'Thirty.'

'Right!' yelled Eddy Hair. 'And how pretty their holiday snaps must look. One point to Manor Road. Next question to the home team. And here it is. "Every room in my house has as many old women in it as there are rooms altogether. Every old woman knits as many knee-warmers as there are old women. I share the knee warmers out among seven of my worst enemies, giving each the same number and as many as possible, and I still have more than enough to cover my knees. How many have I got?"'

Dinah picked up the red pepperpot in front of her and stared thoughtfully at its black stripes, but she did not bother to write anything down. 'Six,' she said in an unhappy voice.

The Headmaster gave a pleased smile as the scores drew level and Lloyd felt a cold shudder creep up his back. Only another nine questions each. And if they were no more trouble than that one, how could Dinah help winning?

But he had not counted on Alec Bates. Alec was the only one of the Manor Road team who seemed to have any brains at all, but he was crammed with them. Every time Eddy Hair asked him a question, he gave the same conceited grin and scribbled away furiously on his piece of paper. And, every time, his answers were right. When the score stood at 8–8, Lloyd suddenly realized that it could be a draw. What would happen then? The Headmaster had obviously realized it too. He was frowning and staring at Alec as the next question was asked, as if he were willing him to fail.

'Right, Smart Alec,' Eddy Hair said sarcastically, 'how about this one? "I have a certain number, made up entirely of sevens. One seven after another. And I can divide it by a hundred and ninety-nine. I want you to give me the last four figures of the answer. But – and here's the catch, folks – I'm not going to tell you how *many* sevens make up the number."'

Alec stared at him.

Eddy Hair did not say anything else. Just turned and looked at the big clock behind him where the second hand was ticking round from 30 to 0. 'Five seconds left,' he said at last. 'Come on, Genius. What's the answer?'

'I – I don't know,' Alec said, as the bell sounded. He did not sound embarrassed. Only furious.

'And the score is *still* 8–8!' Eddy Hair jumped off his barrel and turned a quick cartwheel. 'Goodness me, the excitement's mounting here. What about our other genius? Will she be able to answer her question?'

Dinah looked at him, white-faced, and beside her the Headmaster smiled triumphantly. She gripped the pepperpot hard between her hands, until the knuckles showed white, and glanced across at Lloyd and Harvey, Mandy and Ingrid. When she answered the question, Lloyd could almost feel her reluctance. The score was 9–8 to them, now.

'My, my!' Eddy Hair looked out over the Hall and then raised his eyebrows at the Headmaster. 'What a quiet lot of children you have here. It's the first time your team has gone into the lead. Why aren't they cheering?'

The Headmaster shrugged. 'They can cheer if you want them to.' He raised a hand and instantly, obediently, all the children in the Hall started to cheer loudly and enthusiastically. Then he dropped his hand and they stopped. At once.

Eddy Hair gave him an odd look. 'That's remarkably well organized. I've never seen a school like it.' He grinned at the camera, baring his uneven yellow teeth. 'It's a good thing these bossy teachers don't run the country, isn't it, folks? They'd have us all doing just what they want. Like robots. And where would I be then?'

He chortled merrily. But the Headmaster's face gave a sudden, irritated twitch.

And all at once, Lloyd understood! That was it. That was what the Headmaster wanted. To run the whole country, so that it was as organized and joyless as the school. So that everything was neat and tidy and there was no freedom. He looked frantically at Dinah, wishing there were some way he could tell her.

But, as his eyes met hers, he knew that there was no need to tell her. She had understood too. Her mouth had dropped open and her eyes were stretched wide, in complete horror. As the cameras turned towards the Manor Road team, waiting for their next question, she began to mouth furiously at Lloyd.

'That's what the prefects were talking about,' she said soundlessly. 'He's got them all set up to move people into work camps and –' Her mouthing became faster and more desperate, and Lloyd lost track of what she was saying. But he did not need to know any more. It was too terrible even to think about. It would be like having school everywhere, with no escape.

The Headmaster had seen her, too. He frowned and pointed down into the Hall, straight at the members of S P L A T. Then he looked at Dinah, his eyebrows raised in a question. Miserably, she shook her head. Lloyd could just imagine how trapped she was feeling. Now she knew what the plan was, she could still do nothing to stop it. Not without killing them all.

And there was not much time left. Alec had answered his last question and was grinning again.

'So the score is 9–9,' Eddy Hair said. He ran his fingers through his curls. 'The tension is killing me. Will it be a draw? Everything hangs on the last question.'

Lloyd looked anxiously at Dinah. She was gripping the pepperpot so hard that he wondered it didn't crack and she looked as though she were about to burst into tears.

'So,' Eddy Hair bellowed. 'Here we go. And it's a complicated one, so listen carefully. "I woke up and found I had lost my memory. I couldn't even remember what year it was. So I asked a man who was walking past. He told me: if you multiply my age now by twice my age next birthday, you will get the number of the year we are in. And I can tell you that I don't remember Queen Victoria, but I hope to live to the year two thousand." Got it?'

Dinah nodded. She was just about to open her mouth to give the answer. But before she spoke, she looked across at Lloyd.

And he knew that he could not let her do it. Even if it meant being killed. The idea of having the whole country run by the Headmaster, for ever, was too horrible. Frantically, he shook his head, over and over again, until it felt as though it would fall off his neck.

Dinah shut her mouth again.

'Come on.' Eddy Hair looked at the clock. 'You can have a clue if you like. You only score half a point then, but that's enough to let you win. Do you want the clue?'

'Give it to her!' The Headmaster said sharply. He was looking incredulously at Dinah.

'The clue is this.' Eddy Hair looked down at his piece of paper. ' "By the way," the man added, "I'm not quite as old as my cousin, Winston Smith." Got it?'

Dinah nodded sadly, as though that fitted in with what she thought, but she still did not say anything.

Glaring at her, the Headmaster looked down at the children in the Hall and cleared his throat, as if he were about to speak. Lloyd braced himself. Here it came. The end. *Sorry, H*, he thought, *I couldn't protect you after all. This is more important.*

Then, from the other side of Dinah, came an excited yelp. Lucy, who had sat silently in her chair all through the Quiz, was bouncing up and down.

'I know the answer!' she yelled. 'I know it. Winston Smith's the name of the man in that funny book you told me about, Dinah! It's nineteen eighty-four!'

'That's the right answer,' Eddy Hair said gleefully. 'Well done, Tich. You've saved the day.'

As the giant panda appeared behind the chair of Manor Road's Headmaster, Lloyd began to shake uncontrollably.

Their own Headmaster had reached up and taken off his glasses. Ready for his turn to speak.

CHAPTER 16

'Look into My Eyes'

'That's dealt with the losers,' said Eddy Hair cheerfully, as the Headmaster of Manor Road tried to unwind the eels that the giant panda had tipped over his head. 'Now, how about the winners? A fantastic performance. Not a question missed. Come on, Headmaster. Tell us how you do it.'

With a feeling of sick defeat, Dinah saw the cameras swivel, pointing towards the Headmaster. He smiled into them, his large green eyes alight, and said softly, 'If you all look into my eyes, I will tell you. You must be feeling ready for some sense after all the crazy mess of this show. You must be longing to have everything sorted out tidily, everything settled for you.'

For ever, thought Dinah. *For ever and ever.* Oh, how could she stop what was going to happen? If she did not, life would never be worth living again. But if she tried, it would mean death for everyone else in SPLAT. She could see Lloyd leaning sideways now, whispering to them, explaining what was about to take place. And, as they understood, they all gasped.

'You are all feeling exhausted by the mess,' the Head-master was saying into the camera. 'Tired and weary and ready to sleep . . .'

Through her misery, Dinah felt the familiar sleepiness start to creep over her. And all over the country, people sitting in front of their televisions began to nod over their cups of tea, wondering why they were suddenly yawning.

'. . . you can hardly keep your eyes open. With every second that passes, your eyelids are growing heavier and heavier . . .'

Millions of cups of tea, in homes everywhere, dropped to the ground unheeded as people slumped forwards in their chairs. In the Hall, the audience nodded and Dinah's eyes began to close. She struggled hard to keep them open, but the lids dropped irresistibly.

Then, just before they finally shut, she saw Harvey leap to his feet. He was pointing straight at her, pointing to the table in front of her. Muzzily, she looked at his lips, trying to see what it was that he was mouthing. If only she did not feel so tired . . .

Harvey wagged his finger, pointing in a frenzy. And at last she managed to make out what it was he was saying.

'In your hand!'

Funny, she thought sleepily. Why was he interested in her hand? She looked down, forcing her eyes to stay open for a second longer. Oh yes, she thought vaguely. She was still clutching that silly red pepperpot with the black stripes.

'. . . so, so, *so*, sleepy . . .'

She gave a huge, exhausted yawn. Pepper? she thought. Then – *pepper*!

That was it! Dragging together all the energy she could muster, she forced herself agonizingly to her feet, wrenched the bottom off the pepperpot and flung the contents, as hard as she could, straight into the Head-master's face. Then she sank back on to her chair, knowing that she could not do anything more to resist that creeping, soothing voice.

But what had happened to the voice? It had stopped. For a moment there was silence, and she turned her head slowly sideways.

The Headmaster had gone purple in the face, his lips pressed tightly together, his green eyes bulging ludic-rously. As she watched, his mouth was forced uncon-trollably open in an enormous, a stupendous, sneeze.

'A – A – A – TCHOO!'

As though the strength of the sneeze had blown away her sleepiness, Dinah suddenly found herself wide awake. And, right across the country, people in easy chairs sat up and looked in bewilderment at the spilt tea on their carpets. In the Hall, everyone stirred and gazed in amaze-ment at the sneezing Headmaster. His nose streamed, his mouth gaped ridiculously and his head jerked backwards and forwards.

'Atchoo! Atchoo! Atchoo!'

Then, from all over the Hall, unbelievably, came the sound of laughter. All the children were laughing at the Headmaster. Dinah could see the powerless rage in his eyes, but he could do nothing to stop them. From time to time he tried to speak. He managed to stutter out, 'Des – des – des –' in an effort to give his command to destroy the straw dolls, but every time he got as far as that, another huge sneeze overtook him, and he collapsed.

Eddy Hair was gazing at him ecstatically, as if a sneezing headmaster was what he had always wanted on his show. Raising his voice, he said, above the noise of the sneezes and the laughing, 'Well, folks, beat that if you can for a way to run a school! You know what I always say about this show – *you never know what's going to happen next!*' As the final music began, he winked at the audience and cartwheeled away across the stage.

The Headmaster was just beginning to be able to control his sneezes. He pulled a spotless handkerchief out of his pocket, mopped his face and glared at Dinah with total hatred.

'Do you realize what you have done, you stupid girl?' he gasped. 'You have destroyed this country's chance of becoming the first properly organized, truly efficient country in the world.'

'No I haven't,' she said happily. 'I've saved it from being a miserable place full of scared robots, like this school. And I'm going to think of a way of saving the school from you, as well.'

'The school?' The Headmaster jumped to his feet and waved a scornful hand at the rows of giggling children. 'That rabble? Do you think – a – a – tchoo! – that I want to go on wasting my talents merely looking after *them*? When you've made a laughing-stock of me? A – a – tchoo! I shall resign at once, and let them all sink back into chaos.'

'What are you going to do, then?' Dinah said quietly.

He stood over her, glaring down. For a moment she was afraid that he was actually going to strangle her, in front of everyone. His large hands jerked, and his face was a mask of rage. Then he took a deep breath, and an unpleasant smile spread across his lips. 'Do you think I shall be so foolish as to tell you my plans? No, Miss Clever Glass. You must find them out for yourself. *If* you are clever *enough*. You have defeated me this time, but I know I was meant for greatness. I shall succeed in the end!'

With a loud, scornful laugh, he stalked off the stage and began to stride down the Hall, between the chairs. As his black-clad figure went by, the children stopped laughing and glanced fearfully at him. He did not look either to the right or to the left, but passed them like a tall shadow.

Halfway down the Hall, he suddenly stopped, his body shaking.

'A – a – a – TCHOO!'

As if they had been released from a spell, the children began to giggle again, and Lloyd and Harvey grinned happily up at Dinah, while Ian, Mandy and Ingrid jumped up and danced a jig.

But Dinah did not grin back. She found that her hands were trembling, and she followed the Headmaster with her eyes, all the way, until the Hall door closed behind him.

'How did the show go?' Mrs Hunter said, opening the door. 'We were going to watch it, of course, but I'm afraid we had a – visitor.'

'It was fabulous! Marvellous!' Lloyd said jubilantly, bouncing into the house. 'We –'

'Can you save it?' his mother said, frowning slightly. 'We want you all to come into the sitting room. There's something we've got to talk to you about. Then you can tell us *all* about it.'

Lloyd winked at Dinah behind his mother's back. 'She'd get a shock if we did, wouldn't she?' he mouthed.

Dinah winked back happily, and walked into the sitting room. And stopped abruptly. There, on the settee, was Miss Wilberforce, looking solemn.

'Hallo, Dinah.'

'Hallo, Miss Wilberforce,' Dinah said, in a cold little voice.

Miss Wilberforce sighed, and looked at Mr and Mrs Hunter. 'I'm afraid you're right,' she said. 'It doesn't look as though she feels at home at all. And I was so *sure* she'd feel happy and relaxed here.'

'I don't think it's her fault,' Mr Hunter said sternly. 'I blame the boys.'

Lloyd stared round at them. 'What do you mean?

What are you all talking about?'

'We're talking about Dinah.' Mr Hunter smiled apologetically at her. 'Mrs Hunter and I like having you here, dear. We've grown fond of you. But you don't seem to get on with the boys. You've been at each other's throats all the time, haven't you? So we've agreed with Miss Wilberforce that it would be better for everyone if you went back to the Children's Home.'

Dinah felt as though someone had hit her with a large lump of very cold ice. Her face stiffened. 'Yes, Mr Hunter,' she said, in a small voice.

'But you can't –' burst out Harvey. He stopped and looked helplessly at Lloyd.

Lloyd sat down deliberately in a chair and looked round at the grown-ups. 'I think you're all mad,' he said loudly. 'Why ever do you want to send Dinah away? Plum-coloured pumpkins! We want her here. For ever and ever. I think Mum and Dad ought to adopt her properly.'

Mr and Mrs Hunter goggled, their mouths dropping open. 'You like her?'

'Well, of course,' Lloyd said, as if it were a ridiculous question. 'I think she's fantastic. Except –' he grinned across at her '– except for being a bit thick, of course.'

Dinah had gone rather pink, and was staring at her feet. She did not speak until Miss Wilberforce said gently, 'Well, Dinah? How do you feel about it?'

In a choking voice, as though she could hardly speak, Dinah said, 'Please. Oh please.'

'*That*'s all right, then,' Lloyd said in a satisfied tone.

'Now *please* can we have something to eat? We're all absolutely starving.'

His mother looked at him in bewilderment. 'But you took a packed tea to school. You can't be hungry again. Whatever have you been up to?'

Lloyd, Harvey and Dinah looked at each other and grinned.

'Oh, nothing much,' they said. In perfect unison.

AFTERWORD

He's a monster, of course. No sensible person would ever want to meet someone like him . . . except, that is, on a television screen or in a theatre or, best of all, through the pages of a book:

'Slowly, he climbed the steps up to the stage and turned to look down on the crowded hall below him. There was no need for him to call for silence. Everyone, teachers and children alike, was gazing at him. With a thin smile, he reached up and took off his glasses and his huge green eyes stared out at them.'

And immediately we, the readers, are in his power too – not just Dinah and the other children in this strange Assembly which is so different from any we've ever attended. Yet it is just enough like the real-life version to send a tingle of horror up our spines.

This blending of fantasy and reality is one of the strengths of Gillian Cross's story. After all, the tale of a power-hungry head teacher who hypnotizes his pupils as a springboard for national domination is, quite literally, incredible. Or it would be if the writing weren't so skilful and the supporting detail so cunning. Remember, for instance, how Gillian Cross uses something as simple and precise as a pinprick to make sure she's hypnotized us as well as Dinah. Dinah may have 'floated away on a great tide of sleep', but, more importantly, the reader has also floated away on a great tide of story.

So how did such a spellbinding and fast-paced tale, about a character who's improbable yet all too believable, come to be written?

In fact, *The Demon Headmaster* originated in another book altogether, as Gillian Cross explains:

'The idea . . . came from the bit in *Save Our School* where Clipper writes about the wicked headmaster. My daughter, Elizabeth, who was eight, said "I really like the story of Clipper's about the headmaster. It's much better than the sort of books you write. Why don't you write a story about a wicked headmaster?" And she went on and on about it.'

So Gillian Cross did . . . though it wasn't easy. In her early drafts she tangled up her plot by making Harvey a fantasy character as well – a shape-shifter, no less, who could transform himself into objects like tape-recorders and teapots. It was only when she dropped this complication and began a long process of re-writing that the clear and convincing final version eventually emerged. Even today, though, she still has her doubts. 'Perhaps, after all,' she says, '*The Demon Headmaster* would be a better book if Clipper had written the whole thing.'

Is Gillian Cross just being modest?

Not quite . . . she's simply pointing out how much her story depends on the sort of popular entertainment that's enjoyed by both adults *and* children but with which children may have an advantage – comics, television and the slapstick of circus and pantomime. This is most obvious in the scenes involving Eddie Hair, but if you look carefully you will also pick up other hints – Lloyd's colourful language, for instance, or the school setting, which is more dream-like than realistic, or SPLAT which could have come straight from a tale about Enid Blyton's *Famous Five*. Are we being warned that there are different forms of hypnotism all round us? Gillian Cross seems to be reminding us that the television programmes we watch, the music we listen to and the magazines and books we read (including *The Demon Headmaster*) may all affect our opinions and attitudes . . . so we'd better be as brave and sharp-witted as Dinah and as steadfast as Lloyd, Harvey, Ian, Mandy and Ingrid if we're to keep so many 'hidden' bullies at bay.

At one level, then, *The Demon Headmaster* is a gripping adventure story of a traditional kind in which everything works out well. Look deeper, though, and some highly important issues are also raised – about social control, about the law of the land and about discipline and creativity – all of which are explored with great openness and honesty.

A writer for adults called George Orwell covered much the same ground in his book *1984*, which is mentioned right at the end of the Great School Quiz. George Orwell is careful to avoid any hint of an easy, comfortable ending for his hero, Winston Smith. Gillian Cross makes her ending just as scary:

The Demon Headmaster

'. . . Dinah did not grin back. She found that her hands were trembling, and she followed the Headmaster with her eyes, all the way, until the Hall door closed behind him.'

And come back he does, of course, in her sequels *The Prime Minister's Brain*, *The Revenge of the Demon Headmaster*, and *The Demon Headmaster Strikes Again*. There are some evil figures, it seems, that human beings will never shake off. Thank heavens we've got a Demon Author or two, like Gillian Cross, to show us how to send them into a sneezing fit!

Chris Powling

Puffin | Modern | Classics

ADVENTURES OF THE LITTLE WOODEN HORSE
Ursula Moray Williams

BRIDGE TO TERABITHIA
Katherine Paterson

THE CHILDREN OF GREEN KNOWE
Lucy M. Boston

A DOG SO SMALL
Philippa Pearce

THE DOLPHIN CROSSING
Jill Paton Walsh

GRINNY
Nicholas Fisk

THE MOUSE AND HIS CHILD
Russell Hoban

MRS FRISBY AND THE RATS OF NIMH
Robert O'Brien

THE SILVER SWORD
Ian Serraillier

SMITH
Leon Garfield

STIG OF THE DUMP
Clive King

THUNDER AND LIGHTNINGS
Jan Mark

Retail price £5.99 each

See over for details of how to order

Puffin | Modern | Classics

To order any of the books listed please send a cheque or postal order (payable to Penguin Books Ltd) for the total sum due to:

Puffin Modern Classics
PO Box 69
Leighton Buzzard
Bedfordshire
LU7 7ZD

Please include a list of the title/s and quantity/ies required as well as details of the address that they are to be delivered to.

Alternatively, you may use the credit card hotline for Visa and Mastercard purchases:

01525 – 851 945

Note that a booking charge of fifty pence per order will be made for credit card payments.

Postage and packaging is free for this offer only.

Allow 30 days for delivery (subject to availability of stock).
Offer open to residents of UK only.
This offer is only open until April 1999.

ADVENTURES OF THE LITTLE WOODEN HORSE
Ursula Moray Williams

The Little Wooden Horse is Uncle Peder's finest creation, but when no one wants to buy him, he stays with his master and the two become great friends.

When the toymaker grows poor and ill the brave little horse sets out to sell himself. The Little Wooden Horse has adventures galore whilst trying to make enough money to return to his beloved master.

BRIDGE TO TERABITHIA
Katherine Paterson

It was Leslie who invented Terabithia – the secret country on an island in the dry creek. Here Jess could be strong, unafraid and unbeatable.

So when something terrible happens, Jess finds he can face grief and disaster better than he could ever have imagined.

THE CHILDREN OF GREEN KNOWE
Lucy Boston

Tolly isn't looking forward to spending Christmas with his great-grandmother in her strange house, but as soon as he arrives at Green Knowe he is delighted by the very special kind of magic he finds all around him. Far from being lonely, Tolly is caught up in a wonderful adventure with the other children who have lived there, eagerly learning all about the mysterious house and its delightful secrets.

Puffin | Modern | Classics

A Dog So Small
Philippa Pearce

For months, Ben Blewitt has been thinking about dogs. Alsatians, Great Danes, mastiffs, bloodhounds ... so imagine his disappointment when, for his birthday, Ben receives not a dog but a picture of a dog.

Ben's imagination soon gets to work, though, and that's when his strange adventures begin.

The Dolphin Crossing
Jill Paton Walsh

Pat and his friend John both know the risks they are running in taking a boat across the Channel in the spring of 1940. But they also know they have to do something to help the British soldiers stranded in Dunkirk. Their story makes intensely gripping reading.

Grinny
Nicholas Fisk

Tim and Beth have never heard of their Great Aunt Emma before, so they're shocked when she suddenly appears, grinning, on their doorstep.

Soon they make a horrifying discovery: this old woman is as dangerous as a time -bomb, and she has a fearful task to perform which involves them.

Puffin | Modern | Classics

THE MOUSE AND HIS CHILD
Russell Hoban

Once they are bought and leave the safety of the toy
shop, the clockwork mouse and his child begin their
search for the beautiful doll's house they had
once known.

But, always on their track, determined to destroy them,
is the evil Manny Rat.

MRS FRISBY AND THE RATS OF NIMH
Robert C. O'Brien

Time is running out for Mrs Frisby, who must move
her family of mice before the farmer destroys their
home. But her youngest son is so ill she is convinced
he won't survive the move. Help comes in the
unexpected form of some super intelligent rats, and
little by little Mrs Frisby learns the
rats' extraordinary secret.

THE SILVER SWORD
Ian Serraillier

This is the story of four children's struggle to stay alive
throughout the years of Nazi occupation and,
afterwards, their epic journey from war-torn Poland to
Switzerland in search of their parents.

Based on a true story, this is an extraordinarily moving
account of life during and after the Second World War.

SMITH
Leon Garfield

Smith was a pickpocket – and a very accomplished one at twelve years old.

But the instant he empties the pockets of a certain old gentleman, he finds himself caught up in a dangerous web of murder, intrigue and betrayal.

STIG OF THE DUMP
Clive King

One glorious day the ground gives way beneath Barney and he lands in a cave in the middle of the rubbish dump; and that's when he meets Stig.

Nobody believes his story, but for Barney Stig is totally real, and together they embark on a series of wonderful adventures.

THUNDER AND LIGHTNINGS
Jan Mark

When Andrew's family move house, he strikes up an unexpected friendship with his neighbour, Victor. There isn't a thing Victor doesn't know about the RAF planes flying overhead and the two boys are soon busy tracking their movements.

Andrew is worried when he discovers that Victor's beloved Lightnings are due to be scrapped.

Puffin | Books

For children of all ages, Puffin represents quality and variety – the very best in publishing today around the world.

For complete information about the range of books available from Puffin – and Penguin – please write to:

**Dept. EP
Penguin Books Ltd
Bath Road
Harmondsworth
West Drayton
Middlesex
UB7 0DA**

Or visit us on the worldwide web at:

www.penguin.com